Trigger Warning Issues 1 & 2
Trigger Warning

Caffeinated Muse Press

Consider Yourself Warned

There is a time and a place for trigger warnings. Art isn't one of them. Art is meant to evoke emotion. It shouldn't be shocking for the sake of shock or offense, but it should not be censored. If an artist must give a content or trigger warning before a person reads or experiences the art, the power of the piece is often diminished.

By opening this magazine, you consent to being triggered. You consent to being exposed to art that you might not like or that makes you feel something you weren't expecting or didn't want to feel. Art is about making people feel.

There will be no trigger warnings here.

You will experience the art as it was meant to be read and seen.

Our sincere hope is that at least one piece in this magazine elicits an emotion in you that you didn't expect.

If you don't like what you see, go to our submissions page, and show us what you got.

About the editors

Poetry Editor - Jodie Baeyens

Jodie Baeyens is a single-mother, poet and teaches to support her writing habit. When she isn't trying to find the pen she was just holding, she can be found in the forest dancing beneath the full moon. Originally hailing from New York, she now considers herself a citizen of the world because she has never settled into one place. Her poetry has recently been featured in *Door is a Jar* and in *Peregrine's Fall Journal*. Her forthcoming Chapbook, *Conversations We Never Had*, was the Winner of the 2022 Vibrant Poet Award. Follow her writing at or on Facebook at . '

Fiction Editor - Amy Fenster

Amy Fenster is a novelist, screenwriter, coffee enthusiast and wrangler of small children. She has a Master's degree in creative writing and uses it to subdue unruly characters. Amy began writing at the age of three and has written several screenplays and novels. She writes women's fiction, which is a fancy way to say she does not stick to one genre, but her focus is always to create strong female characters. Amy grew up in New York, but now lives in a paradisiacal land known as San Diego, California. Her hobbies include playing Barbies, Wiccan rituals, keeping small children and animals alive, lots of coffee and trying to stay up past 10:00 PM.

Art Editor - George L Stein

George L Stein is a New Jersey photographer shooting in the art, urban and rural decay, street, alt/portrait, and surreal genres. He has been previously published in Tofu Ink Arts, Sunspot Lit, Wrongdoing Magazine, and Fatal Flaw, among others. Online: insta @steincapitalmgmt, @georgelstein and @darkmuse, as well as .

A person and a swan swimming in water

John Tustin

JUST JILL

Her name is just Jill

and she'll correct you if you call her Jillian.

She's separated now

and it's all a goddamned mess

and she's working 43 hours a week in a fast-food restaurant

to make ends meet

but the ends still aren't meeting.

It's still going wrong;

it's still coming apart,

just a little more slowly now.

The children she works with in the dining room

are arguing about something

and the child who is her supervisor

is crying just out of sight of the people at the drive-thru.

Jill (not Jillian) is keeping it together better than her supervisor

who doesn't have crippling debt and house payments

or a daughter who's stuck in the middle of two angry people

getting one angry divorce.

Suck it up, buttercup!

Get back to supervising so I can finish my shift

and then drive my kid halfway to Dickhead's house

for the every-other-weekend hand-off.

It's getting dark early now.

Jill takes off her name badge,

gets ready to make the drive home.

It's mostly gone wrong but at least she's good at her new job.

It's not sucking the soul out of her –

not quite.

She can do it.

She has to.

She gets into her car and starts to drive

and she begins to cry

and she knows why but she couldn't explain it to you,

not completely,

so there is no point in asking her.

If you do, though,

don't call her Jillian
unless you want her to correct you
because she certainly will.
She stops at the red light,
turns on her music,
gets composed.
The light turns green and she starts driving again.

TRIGGER WARNINGS

"The Indigenous Rainbow Lollipop Review invites one and all to submit their poetry. We believe that tribal fealties and race/sex/gender take precedence over the poem so be sure to tell us all about that. We also insist you provide trigger warnings in your cover letter even though you have no clue what will trigger us. Figure it out."with love,

the editors

Warning!

this poem is about love

this poem is about loss

this poem is about death

and the funerals of cuddly despots

this poem eviscerated a little girl's collection of stuffed animals

this poem is about fat people

who are fat because they eat bad food and too much of it

and that is their own fault

this poem will contain the words

FUCK

CUNT

SLUT

REPUBLICAN

DONALD TRUMP

BITCH

HETEROSEXUAL

this poem will have several pictures of an erect penis

entering the brain of a horny middle-aged woman

this poem will not speak for itself

will not explain or draw a diagram

because this poem hopes you're smart enough

to come to your own conclusion

brave enough to read what makes you uncomfortable

adult enough to crawl out of the womb

of safespace

and read words without getting into the fetal position

and complaining to your college's dean of inclusivity

this poem is sorry your daddy didn't express his love to you

the way you wished he would

this poem is sorry your mommy beat you with a wooden spoon

because you wouldn't finish your supper when you were six years old

but these things

are not the poem's fault

this poem will eschew proper capitalization

punctuation

and also fuck your feelings

this poem is looking at you right now

and hoping you have a reaction

good

or bad

this poem is winking

this poem is crying

this poem is balancing a ball on its nose

and clapping for the reward

of a single fish

this poem is two saggy balls

lying in the wet spot

this poem is based on a true story

the names have not been changed in order to trigger the innocent

I hope you like it

YOU'RE MAKING ME DO THIS

"You're making me do this!" she would exclaim

with less and less drama each time

to her three variously naughty children

and then she would throw the plate against the wall

or put her fist through the plaster

or, worst of all, light up one of the many cigarettes

she had just an hour before sworn to throw away.

"You're making me do this!"

she said to herself in the mirror,

when she thought no one was looking,

unaware that the eyes and ears of children may not always comprehend

but they are always open.

Then she would slap her own face, bite her hand,

shriek at the person she was but understood so little.

"You made me do this,"

her body seemed to say to her eventually –

becoming just skin hanging off a skeleton.

The cigarettes not in sight anymore

but their remains settled into her lungs and her bones,

their old smoke clogging up her blood,

the ashes alive in her smoggy phlegm.

The three children now men

got ready to bury her body

that was moments from packing it in for good.

Some gray putty drying in the holes in the wall;

the mirror she shrieked into covered in a sheet;

all the dishes packed away that she had failed to break.

Thomas Zimmerman (he/him) teaches English, directs the Writing Center, and edits The Big Windows Review at Washtenaw Community College, in Ann Arbor, Michigan. His poems have appeared recently in *hand picked poetry*, *Interstellar Literary Review*, and *Sage Cigarettes*. His latest book is the chapbook *The House of Cerberus* (Alien Buddha Press, 2022). Website: Twitter: @bwr_tom Instagram: tzman2012

So Tonight

you're telling me we live too safe. I flip
the atlas pages. Kiss? You smile, backstabs
and paper cuts are smiling back. Our code
post-post-ironic, half-forgotten songs.
Remember that we're blurry, visions slip
along our shimmer. Hisses, dots, and dabs
we cannot sense are painting us. This road
that's paved with useless dollars, dreamt-up wrongs?
I'll take the wheel, it's better in the ditch.
Here's what we'll do: decide what we're about,
relate these findings to a larger world,
and fashion them to last. We'll have to hitch
our pants up, chill beneath our shadowed doubt,
unpack our dreams: there, reborn We lies curled.

Sister

You're listening to Brahms and reading poems
on your phone, just hoping something warm
will light inside your head, because the weather
everywhere's too dark and cold. It's out
of season, out of joint, a tragedy,
if only life were more heroic. Wine
half gone, you've drawn a picture of a fox:
a journal sketch with ballpoint pen. A spirit
animal, your hippie friend would say.
On morning walks in nearby woods, you've seen
a fox. Last time, she caught your eye. You swear
she read the darkness in you, humped away
into the brush. So much like you: evasion
bears creation. Dare you call her sister?

Bleeding Bite-Sized Pieces

You've cracked a beer, thank God: it's Arrogant

Bastard, a favorite. Your wife's asleep,

TV's on mute. Poetic moment? So

you hope. You've worked all day at paycheck work.

And now, your heart's-blood work, your need to leave

a record. Music streaming from your playlist:

Shostakovich string quartet. The sonnet

and the blackout poem: twin crutches you've

been gimping on. You squirm, the thought-worm bores.

Right: lying fallow is a lie. The dog's

awake and biting on a squeaky toy. Sounds so

much like your verse. You dice a ripe tomato,

world that lies in bleeding bite-sized pieces.

Oh, what title ever captures this?

Weaker

Mommy says never hit back
Mommy says report them to the teacher
but I report them to Mrs. Higginbottom
and Mrs. Higginbottom laughs.

Mommy says never hit back
Mommy says sticks and stones
but they poke the giant pimples of my earlobe
they jab my neck with pencils and pens
and call me faggot, sissyfag, queerbait.

I'm Fifi the French poodle
they go for my brown briefcase
they swarm they work to peel
my fingers off the old brown briefcase
with the wishbone inside.
Don't they know about Cherished
the tiniest pup ever
and my splendid Bar Mitzvah at the Fairmont
that the grown-ups loved
and Willie Mays almost attended
all the caviar
and my room with paintings and a tiger skin rug
and five hundred classical albums?
To them I'm Fifi.
To me I'm Fifi.

One of them asks to see my jack-o'-lantern
and smashes it on the foursquare court.

"Mrs. Higginbottom please isn't there anything you can do?"
She's angry, "Learn to grow up."
And walks away shaking her head.

At recess Dominic Garfono is on me
both hands squeezing my neck
deflating red balloon in a hurry this world closes,

it almost doesn't hurt.

San Franzisko, 1969

In holy German-English
my Mami und Deddi shout
they hit slap smack kick.
I beg them to stop they won't
stop my Mami und Deddi
spit hot old-time German-Jewish
"You hev no cless"
"Shall we call it quit?"
In nearby row houses
Americans behave modern
their language cold.
Why couldn't Gott
have given me cool parents
instead of loving ones
that kick slap and yell?

Our Kristallnacht: destruction
rips me from dreamland into
blood and broken glass.
Mami threw an ashtray
couldn't take the torrent of gripes.
His eyeglasses in ruins
blood on the comforter.
Then bandages cover his nose,
weeks of no sound in the house
but the clattering of
old-time plates.
I pray to Gott for peace
Gott, I know I'm bad
and that's why they fight.
Meek is the way
Mami und Deddi want me
in loving German-English.

One night Mami gets tipsy
swallows many pills.
Deddi shakes her can't wake her

Deddi rushes past the red lights
sirens after us
all the way to Mt. Zion.

A trip to Lake Berryessa
to watch the moon landing.
Mami und Deddi hug
in our mobile home.
By a fetid pond, peace.
At dinner Mami und Deddi
they're hitting slapping kicking
cussing and smashing
voices brimming with high-pitched
anger English.

So all Vitalis-slick
I knock on the principal's door.
Miss Tennessee Bentley
loves that I'm an early bird.
I tell all about the quarrels at home.
"But they adore you
and they mean well, Alex.
Think what they went through in Germany."
She looks like Tennessee Tuxedo
birdlike, efficient, erect.

That night Mami yells
"The child het to go cry at Miss Bentley!
See how you destroy."

White Christmas
flickers into my room
Bing Crosby carefree on the slopes
snow warm against my cheeks.

To Drain the Eye and Shape It Like a Paradise

Nineteen hours I stayed in Myles.

I nutted eighteen times,

he was a blackjack dealer, Adonis of the trailer park

with fourteen cats aided by the Cat Foundation.

Part Hawaiian part German part Portuguese.

Myles Machado, meth addicted and positive.

Nineteen hours boffing Myles raw.

He lingered so long in the fetid AIDS ward

of Patriot Benito Mussolini Hospital and Clinic

his friends stopped visiting and his cats starved.

Someone inserted a blackjack table into his corpse

and called him the perfect coffin slave.

Myles feared ovens so he was buried unburned

except his nipples went to rest at a Ritz

his navel at a Hilton, his pinkies at Madame Tussauds.

Since he was a TV addict they showed graveside Fox News.

TV blabbered night and day and loved itself

the way a fetus loves itself for its insanity.

I stroked at his grave hungry for a replica of the deceased.

Where else could I nut eighteen times in nineteen hours?

Such birth smacks of evil so I consulted an Algerian

who built red crows and mice that played the tuba

as well as other projects that'll surely break the world.

His Myles replicant was garbage.

The new Myles had a garbage voice and garbage hair

and especially his hole smelled like garbage.

I had them recreate the trailer, the fourteen cats.

Half the night I tried to plug the replicant raw.

Half a year later I'm in the fetid AIDS ward

of Patriot Benito Mussolini Hospital and Clinic

minus my pinkies, nipples and navel.

They've made my room a South Seas island

and for company gave me a mink and a goldfish.

Someone sold my left hand and foot.

I'm flowing with other bodies off Hawaii.

Rabbis and attorneys flow with me.

Blind giggles.

James Mulhern's writing has appeared in literary journals over two hundred times. In 2013, he was a Finalist for the *Tuscany Prize in Catholic Fiction*. In 2015, Mr. Mulhern was awarded a writing fellowship to Oxford University. That same year, a story was longlisted for the *Fish Short Story Prize*. In 2017, he was nominated for a *Pushcart Prize*. His novel, *Give Them Unquiet Dreams,* is a *Readers' Favorite Book Award* winner, a *Notable Best Indie Book of 2019,* a *Kirkus Reviews* Best Book of 2019, and a RED RIBBON WINNER, highly recommended by *The Wishing Shelf Book Awards* in the United Kingdom.

The Crosswalk

Today I saw a father and son
stepping onto the crosswalk.
I braked and watched them pass.
Son on father's shoulders,
headed to the park with swings.
I drove on, thinking of you
and wondered why you
never lifted me and held my legs
or brought me to the swings.
But you were not that type of father.
Once, we built a shed together.
I heard you say at a family party years later,
"Remember when Danny and I built the shed."
But it wasn't my brother
who cut wood and hammered nails with you.
I was bothered just a bit.
I had other memories,
like when you held my hands as we knotted my tie,
how we both looked in the mirror,
and I saw myself in your face.
You patted my shoulders.
Someone crossed the room and paused to take a picture.
It was on the table by your coffin. Your hands on mine.
Proof that we had closeness for a moment,
and that is enough.

Piano

On that gray day, you chopped the grand piano with an ax.

Surrounded by yellow and red leaves on the hard earth,

you raised your arm to smash it all apart.

I could only wonder. You were a man raised to think

crying was weak. Strength and power should define you.

Men like you could not voice their secrets or despair.

You shattered the instrument, exorcising its shiny veneer.

Resin-impregnated paper, dovetail joints, wooden ribs,

and polished mahogany scattered around you.

Slowly the curved outline of the piano became a ragged mess.

The soundboard heart cracked. Small planks of air-dried wood

joined the miscellany of strings, keys, and padded hammers.

I thought of my mother, the day she moved out,

how you changed the locks and emptied every closet,

destroying each vestige of your shared lives.

If I had left the window to join you outside,

I would have seen your tears,

glistening strings on the soundboard of a broken soul.

Brother

On our way to the dance, we made a fire under the bridge.

Snow fell outside the darkness of our shadowed space.

We sang about the bottles of beer we raised with gloved hands.

You lay your arm over my shoulders. Your face glowed in the flames.

Twigs crackled and bits of paper rose in the smoke.

Snow glistened under the streetlights beyond the bridge.

In a while we'd step into the cold brightness but for now

I loved the dark space, the circle of fire, and our song.

In the blackness of my bedroom, sometimes a fire

blazes and I see our pink faces before the flames.

I hear our voices and the sighing of the wind.

Your arm crosses my cold neck and hugs my shoulder,

and I dream we never stepped outside our hallowed space.

The snow was so cold and the streetlights too strong.

Brad Rose was born and raised in Los Angeles, and lives in Boston. He is the author of five collections of poetry and flash fiction: ***Pink X-Ray, , Momentary Turbulence,*** , and the forthcoming, ***WordinEdgeWise***. Seven times nominated for a Pushcart Prize, and three times nominated for the Best of the Net Anthology, Brad's poetry and fiction have appeared in, *The Los Angeles Times, The American Journal of Poetry, New York Quarterly, Puerto del Sol, Clockhouse, Folio, Cloudbank, Baltimore Review, 45th Parallel, Best Microfiction 2019, Lunch Ticket, Sequestrum, Right Hand Pointing, Cultural Daily*, and other publications. Brad is also the author of seven poetry chapbooks, among them, *Democracy of Secrets, Collateral, An Evil Twin is Always in Good Company*, and *Funny You Should Ask.*

DEVOTION

No One Left to Blame

Tuesday, at the personality clinic, I noticed the robots were dancing to the stereophonic screams of their artificial intelligence, so I tried to cozy up to one of the cute ones, but before I could get my mind around it, it squeaked, *Washing is one of the most significant things you'll ever do to your clothes.* Admittedly, I'm of out of the loop, but physicists still struggle to fully comprehend the proton. As I understand it, they've got some pretty silly quarks. Of course, you never know for sure, but who doesn't want to have their cake and eat it too? No use getting in over your head. If you do, you might be persuaded to remember events that never really happened, like that time the house caught fire, and you realized there was no one left alive to blame.

No Hard Feelings

Thursday, I found myself downtown, lawyer shopping—no thanks to years and years of positive thinking. Those criminals, you'd think at the rates they charge, they could at least afford to play more than miniature golf. I'm a man of my times and I like loud attention, so I laminated my hair and bushwhacked a couple of sacrilegious church goers. I was told there might even be a little money in it, if you know where to look. While I always try to strive and succeed, I prefer to cultivate my personal space and curate my fire ant farm, although crowds make me nervous—especially tiny red ones. Trixie warned me about the animal tracking devices and the closed-circuit TVs, so I evaded detection for as long as I could by wearing my ambiguous amphibious disguise—the one featuring mindless mindfulness and an airborne shoehorn. Thank goodness, bats are the only flying mammals. Anyway, when I finally appeared before the commissioner of sub-justice on trumped-up charges of uncreative loitering and petty shamanism, he winked at me and said, *Even Jesus could have used a better attorney.* I admire the iron fist of justice. Too bad about all those crucifixions.

The Competition

I'm not sure who, but you remind me of someone—only taller. It runs in my family. One day, I plan to become my own worst frenemy, but until then, I hope to get even with myself by breaking my heart in two. I'm not half the man I used to be. There are 44 murders a day in the US, and roughly $500 million to $1.5 billion collected each year in ransom money. You can imagine how hard it must be for the competition to catch up.

A person and person kissing

Photo Daisy Renee Photography

Karen Beatty   Reared in
Appalachia near the Licking River, Karen Beatty explored the Mekong River as a Peace Corps Thailand Volunteer. Now settled between
the Hudson River and the East River on the Isle of Manhattan, she believes that, like its tidal rivers, New York City perpetually surges
and flows with a diversity of people, places and experiences that serve up all manner of gifts to those open to receive. Karen's short stories
and essays appear in <u>Eureka Literary Magazine,</u> <u>Snowy Egret,</u> <u>Books Ireland,</u> and, most recently, in the <u>Mud Season Review</u>.

Passing Karma

Too soon for him

The time has come

When I must never again

Cater, scramble

And comply

In acquiescence

To his neediness

INCONCEIVABLE

Pulsing turns to pounding

Trembling, cold

Dread of acknowledgment

Once again an empty womb

Lost And Not Found

Secretly abused child with class rage and no body to speak of.

Paula Frew - An Ohio native, the author wrote her first poem, Daffodils, in the fourth grade. At that time, she fell in love with the form. She wrote through the angst of adolescence and into the beauties and dissonance of adulthood. She has been published in several journals and anthologies.

Metamorphosis
The caterpillar
Spins a cocoon.
Will he be moth
Or butterfly?
Regardless,
He will fly!

the fix

friendship

long and true.

wrecked

harsh and strong.

repaired

humble, and gentle.

Child-like Wonder

A billion

stars, painted

with a sharp brush,

light the night

at Grandpa's

country farm.

A billion

fluffy clouds

created by the

jets flying

over Grandpa's farm.

A billion

grains of sand,
rocks fragmented
by a giant's feet
populate the beach
around Grandpa's pond.
A billion
raindrops cried
by angels above
drive me inside
at Grandpa's house.
A billion
memories crafted
in an innocent child
by a creative
man, who loved
his granddaughter.

William Doreski lives in Peterborough, New Hampshire. He has taught at several colleges and universities. His most recent book of poetry is *Dogs Don't Care* (2022). His essays, poetry, fiction, and reviews have appeared in various journals.

Our friend spilled a thundering pot
of cheese soup that scorched to bone.
That's why her hand is bandaged.
We worry that infection will douse
her manual vigor, but smiling
off the danger she proceeds.
The day looks sick with ice and sleet.
Predictable, predicted, the mess
smirks on every utile surface.
We sit outdoors under the eaves
and savor village geometry
from a safe if chilly outlook.
The rapture that blinds with snow
has yet to arrive. The winter blue
that soothes with gendered strokes
withholds until Christmas has done
its pagan pageantry in suburbs
discolored by repeated beatings.
Vestigial limbs are flailing
to no avail. Our bandaged friend
drives away in her Chevy truck
with her gaze affixed to asphalt
where evolution publicly stalls.
North or south, magnetic fields
whimper with miniature frights.
We could abandon our shelter
and walk abroad in a shower
but we'd lose our credibility.
Let's stop reading politics
as weather. No point distorting
vanishing-point perspective
to explain the third-degree burn
waving goodbye in the distance.

Fuseli's Grimace

In the bruise of night a figure
mutters about astronomy
while placing her hands on me
with graven pneumatic force.
You sleep right through this event,

your face turned to the blankest wall.
The figure doesn't intend
to compete with you but braces
her smile against the writhing dark
and pries me open, exposing
crystals sculpted by chemistry
that I almost learned in high school.
I would rather have not seen
so far into my interior,
but you refuse to awaken
and intervene. The figure,
formed of molecular erratics,
ravages all over me, slurring
my details and rendering flesh
as obsolete as papyrus.
Does this suggest Fuseli's
grimace reversed so I become
the white horse with flyaway mane
and impossibly pointed ears
and unseeing lightbulb eyes
while the terror is the woman
leering over my clumsy sprawl?
The squatting cat-faced demon
is you enjoying the tableau
while the night bleeds into itself,
deflating and gradually pooling
into conviction tough as bedrock.

Flesh-Runes

Horizons from the Renaissance

crease your face at angles

you've devised over a lifetime.

This look impales the world

on pins and needles depicted

in flesh-runes no one can read.

The wind off the river lingers

in the creases. Last year's phlox

recalls dwindled clusters of bees.

The Unitarian steeple clock

reads half an hour into

a future compressed to flatter

your blue and gray intuitions.

What if the famous man appeared

with his black leather portfolio?

Would you abandon me to etch

your runes all over his body

in a half-abandoned motel?

So many horizons competing

for the mind to cross into shades

of color not quite of this Earth.

Why can't you muffle those runes

and press me to your geography

without the antique discords?

Your horizons break like surf

in mouthfuls of foam. This effect

stifles talk with gasps of erosion.

Your well-honed look savages

the smallest hint of critique

with runes harsh enough to rhyme.

A gated entrance to a building

Paul Lewellan retired from Education after teaching for five decades in the public schools and at small liberal arts colleges. Now he lives and gardens in Davenport, Iowa, with his wife Pamela, his Shi Tzu, Mannie, and their ginger tabby, Sunny. He has recently published fiction in Miniskirt Magazine, DASH Literary Journal, New Croton Review, True Chili, Jupiter Review, and Holy Flea Lit. Although he doesn't believe life begins at 74, it does get more interesting.

Attraction and Taboo

By Paul Lewellan

"Calling the Uber was the responsible thing to do, Clark." My mother-in-law, Allison McQuery, set her purse on the black marble kitchen counter. "Thank you." She stretched up and kissed me on the cheek. The scents of Chanel No. 5 and Bombay Sapphire lingered. "We'll retrieve your car in the morning." She kicked off her shoes. "I'm not ready for the evening to end."

"Then we won't let it," I assured her.

It was a stupid thing to say.

Savannah joined us in the kitchen, shaking off the rain. "I need a drink."

My wife gets right to the point.

"That's the last thing you need, Little Miss Three-Martinis Before Supper," her mother told her. Allison unbuttoned her Burberry trench coat. She removed the matching bucket hat. "I'll make coffee."

"Tonight was supposed to be a celebration," Savannah huffed. "People drink when they celebrate."

"You sound like your father." Allison shook out her thick black hair streaked with gray highlights and draped her coat over a kitchen chair.

"Nothing wrong with that." Savannah shed her raincoat, too, letting it drop to the floor. She kicked her Christian Louboutin four-inch heels under the kitchen table, then shimmied out of her cocktail dress, leaving it in a damp puddle. "He knows how to party." She stood shivering in her bra and half-slip.

"I invited him," I told my wife.

Her mother stated the obvious. "He chose not to come."

Savannah unhooked her damp bra and let it drop. "I'm going to the hot tub, Clark. Bring me a drink."

I paused to formulate an appropriate response. *Nothing. I had nothing.*

My mother-in-law stepped in. "I know where Errol keeps his twenty-five-year-old scotch."

"Mother! Daddy saves that for special occasions."

"I thought this *was* a special occasion. Besides, Iowa is a community property state."

"I can get my own drink." She staggered slightly, then waved me off when I reached out to steady her. Barefoot in her tiny half-slip, she threaded her way to the refrigerator and pulled out a bottle of Ciroc she'd stashed in the freezer. Her last words as she exited through the patio door were, "Don't touch Daddy's Dalmore."

I took a breath and slowly exhaled. My wife was a master of exits and entrances. I reached down to gather up her clothes.

"Leave them, Clark. Let her pick them up in the morning like a responsible adult."

"If only...." *If only she were more like her mother.*

"Why don't you make a fire in the study while I get the Dalmore."

I shook my head. "It would be wasted on me. I can't tell the difference between one scotch and another."

"Of course, you can. My ex-husband never wanted you to try." She winked. "He's not here anymore."

Allison never winked.

It had been an unusual evening. I'd never spent a thousand dollars on a meal before, but the three of us were celebrating new positions. Savannah would be her firm's chief legal counsel because of her boss's resignation after sexual harassment charges. Allison had been appointed Chair of the Sociology department at the Southern Iowa University, following a sabbatical in Guatemala and the campus-wide initiative to diversify department chair positions. I'd been hired as the International Marketing Director at my former firm's chief competitor, a position I'd pursued for years. *No lightweights at tonight's party.*

Allison got glasses while I started the fire. We settled into the Winsor chairs by the fieldstone fireplace. She poured our drinks. "A scotch like this is a privilege. Errol spent $400 on it and never shared it with anyone except his daughter."

I lifted the glass to my lips. "Our turn now." I savored the golden liquid. "Unbelievably smooth...."

"The age makes the whiskey taste better, but it's the wood in the barrels that breaks down the coarser flavors." She drank deeply. "The longer the alcohol stays in the barrel, the smoother it gets."

"Amazing." I took another sip. "Why don't they age all whiskey like that?"

Allison laughed her deep throaty laugh. "Distillers couldn't afford it. By the time a 25-year-old scotch has aged, 40% of what was in the barrels is gone. It's called 'The Angel's Share.' Natural evaporation over time."

"So, it's not expensive because it's old; it's expensive because it's rare." I raised my glass. "A toast to the finely aged and the rare."

She laughed again and drank.

Finally I said, "We can't do this anymore."

Allison swirled the scotch in its tumbler. "Technically, you and I haven't done anything. Some phone calls and emails while I was in Guatemala. Texts after I got back." She emptied the glass. "Never even a stolen...."

As if on cue, my wife entered the study still wearing the half-slip, now plastered to her thighs. "I'm going to bed." Savannah blew me an air kiss. She'd tucked her cellphone under her arm. Her face was flushed. In her hand was the bottle of Ciroc. "Don't keep the old broad up too late." She disappeared up the stairs.

"Always looking out for you," I joked. *Neither of us laughed.*

I handed her my Waterford crystal tumbler and Allison refilled our glasses with the last of the Dalmore. "What do you suppose Savanah was doing out there?"

"Masturbating in your hot tub."

"Clark! You don't know that."

"I wish I didn't. She sent me a video once by accident. She'd meant to send it to Danby."

"Her boss?"

"Ex-boss. You know, if she hadn't made that error...."

"If she'd actually sent it to Danby...." I saw the wave of recognition.

"Iowa Equity and Casualty would have fired her along with him. They suspected there was something between them but couldn't prove it. With a half-dozen potential harassment suits pending, they wanted Danby gone. Replacing him with Savannah ...."

"Made the company appear to care about women...."

"Exactly." *I waited.*

"Can she do the job?"

"She can. Hell, she's your daughter." I lifted the newly refreshed glass. "Unfortunately, she's also her father's daughter, and so she has no moral sense."

"She knows the rules and pretends to follow them, when in truth, breaking them excites her."

Allison's assessment perfectly described my wife. "Taboos pack a charge. The erotic rush is irresistible." I raised my glass again. "To the sociopaths of the world."

"To the sociopaths." She tapped her glass on mine. "Can't live with them. Can't live without them."

"Actually...." I got up and walked to the fireplace. I added another log, which made no sense, since the study already felt like a sauna. *I was stalling.* "I've decided to leave her."

"Why? She's cheated on you before, and you've forgiven her.... What's different this time?"

"She told me she wants to get pregnant."

That wasn't the answer she'd expected. "Savannah would be a lousy mother."

"You weren't."

"She isn't me."

"She is not." I untied my shoes and slid them off, placing them carefully beside the chair where I could find them in the morning. I untied my tie, folded it, and set it on the end table. I removed my sport coat, as Allison stared into the fire. "She and I haven't had sex in six months."

"But...."

"After we found out about my low sperm count, she started recruiting sperm donors." I looked at the remains of the scotch. "She told me I'd had my chance."

Allison stood up and removed her suit jacket. "Don't you think it's warm in here?" *Her question was rhetorical.* She unbuttoned the first two buttons of her silk blouse, plucked the material from her skin, and fanned herself with it. "I wondered why you didn't leave her years ago."

"I couldn't figure out how to stay connected to you, without being married to her. If I walked away, you'd be forced to choose between us."

"And you thought I would have chosen her?" The Westminster chimes announced that it was midnight. "Let's talk about that. I'll make coffee." She started toward the kitchen. "Brandy goes well with coffee. See what Errol has in his liquor cabinet."

"Given what we need to talk about, shouldn't we be sober?"

"Heavens, no. Sober I wouldn't have suggested you spend the night, or that we should raid the scotch. And without the scotch, I'd never do this...." She walked back to me, took my head in her hands, and kissed me, passionate, tender, with the hint of promise.

When she returned a few minutes later with a carafe of coffee and cups, she saw a distinctive bottle on the table. "Louis XIII de Remy Martin. Why the cognac?"

"I found a locked compartment and wondered, if Errol left a $400 scotch out, what would he lock up?"

"But it was locked–"

"It's a liquor cabinet, not a Sentry Safe. It has a key, and the key couldn't be far away. It was the third place I looked."

"Errol has a brilliant legal mind but lacks imagination and is oblivious to security. His password is still 'password'." She cleared away the tumblers as I got up and stirred the fire. "Don't you find it warm here?" She unbuttoned her blouse and dropped it to the floor; her skirt followed. "That's much better."

I picked up the bottle and broke the seal. "What makes this so special?"

"The cognac is aged 50 to 100 years."

"So how much are we paying for the Angel's Share?"

"Best guess, four-grand."

"$4000 a bottle?"

"Yes."

"Maybe we should skip the coffee."

"Good idea." Dressed in her pale gray slip, she took the cognac from me and poured us each a generous portion in the cups. She sat down and crossed her legs. "Now, Clark, where were we?"

"You were telling me about your sabbatical."

"No, I wasn't." She lifted her cup. "I haven't mentioned that at all."

"It's related." She waved her hand over the cup and inhaled the cognac's aroma. I did the same. We sipped in unison. "I stayed in my marriage because I thought it was the only way to stay connected to you."

"Then last year I left to study domestic abuse in Central America."

"The first week in Guatemala City, you emailed me amazing descriptions of the country and insights about the women you'd met."

"And you, who wrote back."

"Within a month we were emailing every night."

"The day Esmerelda's husband doused her with boiling water, I phoned you distraught. I had a six-pack of Gallo beer, a bottle of tranquilizers, and a bottle of Zacapa rum. I wasn't sure I could do the work anymore."

"I was drinking Sam Adams...."

"You talked me through it. You gave me the courage to stay. You were the reason I got through the sabbatical year. Thank you." Allison took another drink and said pointedly, "Clark, don't you think it's warm in here?" *Another rhetorical question.*

"I do." I got up, unbuttoned my shirt, and pulled the tails from the waistband. I dropped my slacks to the floor and stepped out of them. I removed my t-shirt and lowered my boxer shorts. Finally I took off my Bombas.

She stood, lifted her slip up over her head, and set it on the chair. "A little help," she said, turning so that I could undo the clasp of her bra. I touched her bare shoulder and stroked her cheek. She kissed me. I played with her breasts. "Yes... please...more...."

I knelt, ministering to her until she climaxed. She sank to the floor, pulling me down beside her. "I've waited so long...."

Hours later, spent, we fell asleep in each other's arms.

When I woke up, the fire was out. I was naked and shivering. Allison was gone, but standing over me, wearing her father's pajama top with a mug of coffee in each hand, was my wife. "You finally did it. You fucked her. Good for you, Clark. I know you've wanted to for a long time." She handed me a mug. "Mother made a fresh pot. The cinnamon rolls will be out in ten minutes."

"You're pissed."

"Not so much." Savannah motioned toward the kitchen. "You must have brought your A-game last night. She's singing show tunes." She started back to the kitchen. "You should grab a quick shower."

In the guest bathroom I found a man's bathrobe hanging on the door, a toothbrush still in its package, and a fresh disposable razor. In the mirror I saw teeth marks, scratches, and hickeys everywhere.

When I joined the women in the kitchen, Allison was wearing an identical robe. "I hope you're hungry." She suppressed a grin and handed me a mug.

The coffee was dark roasted from Guatemalan beans, purchased from an indigenous growers' co-op where she'd done workshops for abused women, and then at their request, for their husbands. "The males didn't want to listen but were eager to sell their coffee."

Savannah made the cinnamon rolls from a Pillsbury tube. She and I sat in the high-top stools at the breakfast nook looking out over the patio.

When Allison joined us, she told my wife, "You're taking this well."

"I saw it coming." Savannah pulled apart the warm sweet bread, slathered it in butter, and popped a piece in her mouth. She chewed. "You've been mooning over each other since your sabbatical." She pulled off another piece. "How can I blame you? I cut Clark off months ago. You'd been drinking...."

"It wasn't the alcohol," I interjected. Allison touched my arm. "I mean, yes, it lowered our inhibitions...."

"It wouldn't have happened last night if we hadn't already entertained those thoughts. Unnatural acts become natural when played out in your mind."

"Bullshit." Savanah got up and put a slice of wheat bread in the toaster. She pulled out the Super Chunk peanut butter from the pantry and grabbed a knife. "I suppose now you're going to assure me it'll never happened again?"

"No. That's something your father would say. And it's probably not true."

"Really? Well, thanks, Mother. That's swell." Savannah stuffed her mouth with peanut butter toast.

I came to Allison's defense. "Look you're the serial cheater, the wife who cut me off...."

"The one who got everyone drinking at dinner," Allison added, "the one who suggested spending the night." *That's when I realized....*

"You set us up!"

My wife shoved the last bite of toast into her mouth. "Maybe," she mumbled.

Her mother walked out to the patio without a word. At the hot tub, Allison dropped her bathrobe and got in.

I followed, turned on the jets, and joined her. The warm water roiled over us. I closed my eyes. "Why would Savannah push us together?"

"It doesn't matter." She stroked my leg. "What if there were no taboos, no legal, moral, or social restraints...?" When I didn't say anything, she stopped stroking. "It's not a hypothetical question."

"Technically, it is," I argued. "Because there are taboos and social restraints."

"You're both married to someone else, and Daddy wants to come home." *Savannah had come out. She was pissed.* "He said you won't let him in the house."

"It *is* my house." She leaned back against the side of the tub avoiding eye contact.

"It's his house, too."

"No, it isn't. It was a wedding gift from my parents. They liked Errol but didn't trust him. They made him sign a prenup acknowledging my sole ownership. He has no claim."

"Where will he live?"

"Your father asked me the same question. I suggested he move into Tiffany's condo. It's got two bedrooms. He cosigned the lease, and he's already paying the rent."

"Tiffany? His intern?"

"Yes, the one he's been raving about for months."

"The woman who's ten years younger than me?"

"Yes. That's the one," I pointed out. "The one who reminded him of you at that age."

"The bastard! How could he...."

"Stop it, Savannah! Stop it. Listen to yourself," her mother told her. "You had no trouble accepting that he cheated on me, but now that he's cheating on you...."

Savannah stood, incredulous, before the hot tub. "Daddy and I have never.... Not like you and Clark...."

"I think you wanted to...."

"Maybe...."

"Good thing it never happened. He'd have been a disappointment."

"What do you mean...?"

"His metabolism changed. One morning he looked in the mirror saw a middle-aged man, forty pounds overweight, with a beer gut. No one wanted to see him in a Speedo anymore. With the weight came high blood pressure and medication to treat it. The man with the perpetually rock-hard dick suddenly had trouble getting it up. He got self-conscious. That made it worse."

"So how do you explain Tiffany?" I asked.

"A good-looking man with money and position can always get laid if he tries hard enough." Allison winked at me.

"You're disgusting!" My wife appraised the two of us in the hot tub. "Clark, if we divorce, I get the condo. With the promotion, I can afford it. Save me looking for another place."

"What about me?"

"I bet, with Daddy gone, Mother would welcome you." She turned to leave. "And honestly, if you two are happy, I don't know what the big deal is." Savannah started walking into the house. "I'll swing by later with some of your clothes."

"He won't need them for the next couple days," Allison called out as she walked away.

"Don't push it, Mother!" Savannah retreated into the kitchen.

"Are you all right with this, Clark?"

"I am." I took a deep breath and then exhaled. "Maybe later, when we let the world back in, we'll need to talk."

"Plenty of time for that.... Later."

A picture containing person, outdoor, ground, sidewalk

Photo Daisy Renee Photography

Ben Umayam moved to NYC to write the Great American Filipino Gay Short Story. He worked for political pollsters, then became a fancy hotel chef and then retired. He is working that short story again. He was recently published by Querencia Anthology Autumn 2022, The Phare, BULL, Down in the Dirt, Metaworker, Ligeia, EthelZine, Lotus-eaters, 34th Parallel, Digging Through The Fat, Anak Sastra, Corvus Review, and others.

ELPHIA
CHURCH
JESUS
SAVES

Georgy Girl

Georgina is the first St. Stephen's staffer I meet. Father Tom takes me through the kitchen. "We are going to renovate starting next week. You arrived just in time, Ben." Pots and pans are stacked high under a homemade wooden table, many grimy from non-use. Old industrial stove from 1955. The kitchen would be reworked. New everything.

Georgina storms into the kitchen with her lunch dishes. She washes at the sink. Father Tom introduces us. "Georgina, this is Ben, our new chef. He will be cooking dinners for us from now on, every night, Monday through Friday."

"So glad to meet you." She pauses her aggressive washing. "Did you tell him, Father? I worked in a deli. I cook very good!"

Father winks at me and whispers, "She helps out with sandwiches. She doesn't cook." At normal voice, he says, "No, Georgina, I did not tell him. He is in charge of meals at night. This makes him the new kitchen boss."

"Wellllll... how nice to meet you." She looks at me like it is not so nice. "Your name is Ben?"

"*Si, me llamo* Ben. As in *Benhamin. Yo hablo español, pero poquito poquito. Yo trabajo con muchos cocineros latinos.* So, I speak a little kitchen Spanish."

"Ahaaaa, okay, *Benhamin.* Father, do you want that white tuxedo shirt for tomorrow night?" Georgina is an all-around housekeeper for the resident priests. She cleans the living quarters and common areas; she does laundry and irons, a housekeeping Gal Friday. Father answers yes, and she leaves to iron.

It sounds like a lot of work. It isn't, not for her. Four priests live at the priory. Most do their own laundry and clean their own rooms.

Georgina spends most of her time just hanging out. She parks in the laundry room with her cell phone. When someone comes in, she pretends to be ironing or doing another load of laundry.

We bond a little in the beginning. We entertained a lot, dinner parties, and cocktail gatherings. She becomes my expert in setting up the bar. All the liquor is in a closet in the main dining room. It has many shelves, and aside from the two reserved for scotches, vodkas, and sodas, the others are packed with chafing dishes. Instead of clothes on hangers, the closet is full of tablecloths. Another shelf holds the cloth napkins. Various table décor is also found in there, candlesticks and the like.

They also keep the big collection baskets in there, Sunday nights into Monday morning. They no longer use the rectory safe. The former Choir Master had mastered the art of taking money from it. Instead, they move the baskets upstairs into the liquor closet. Seven older ladies volunteer to count every Monday. They count at the big dining table, service for 12. It is easier for these ladies this way. There is an elevator that takes them from the street to the money.

They count a lot of money at St. Stephen's. Masses are packed. At the children's Mass, kids file down to the basement for religious instruction; this takes a full 5 minutes. So many kids, so many parents. All the other masses are pretty full of students from colleges and universities surrounding the church. Most masses in New York have twenty people, forty if you are lucky. Father Tom has brought this church back from the brink; the congregation is now in the hundreds, Sunday attendance, maybe a thousand. Even in Rome, it isn't easy to get more than forty people to Mass on a Sunday. Unless of course, you are the Vatican.

————

They tear up the old kitchen. I cook in the basement. It is a big community center with a huge kitchen. Saturdays, the basement houses the soup kitchen. Other days, groups like AA rent the space. Two types: gay and non-gay. The church is a block away from Christopher Street, NYC's old gay mecca.

I cook down there for a few hours, bring the food up three floors, by the dumb waiter, and serve dinner to the priests in their dining room. Then, after dinner, I leave the dishes in the sink.

After a few days, Georgina confronts me. "Benjamin, you are in charge of the kitchen, *siii*? Why you don't wash the dishes?"

"Georgina, I am the chef. I am here to cook dinner. They hired me for four hours. I cook, serve the food, and clear the table. The rest is for you to do. You are the housekeeper, *siii*?

She raises her voice. "No, Benjamin, I clean for the priest! *No limpio para ti*!"

Father Tom is reading at the kitchen table. He is the boss without being the boss.

"Let me explain. I am a professional trained at a specialty school. I get paid a lot of money because of my training and experience. The priests will not pay me more than $70 an hour to wash dishes."

Given this out, Father Tom is not confrontational. On the contrary, he says to Georgina, "Listen to Ben; he is correct."

"You are right, Georgina. I am in charge of the kitchen. You are the housekeeper. You come in the morning and do their dishes from the night before. You did that before. You still do that. Nothing has changed, except you don't make sandwiches for dinner anymore." She leaves in a huff.

Father continues to read his paper. He holds the paper the old-school way, not folded up like folks do on the subway. His whole face is covered. He speaks into The Arts section. "You talk to her like she is a Latina stereotype. Give her some slack, Ben." I am embarrassed, a Filipino American, priding that I am without a bone of racism in my body. I feel like I am at Confession, Father's comforting voice telling my penance for my sin.

———

Maybe 25 years ago, Georgina escaped Mexico. She hires *coyotes*, people to smuggle her and a cousin out. The smugglers leave them in a desert. They have no water, no food. They tell them to walk towards the light, but it is entirely dark, with no light. They walk and walk in circles. No light, no water, no food. They rest, fall asleep, and wake up. They see the light. Tired and thirsty, they walk, and finally arrive. Someone meets them and puts them on a truck. They fall asleep. When they awaken, they are united with cousins in the States.

She moves to New York and raises a family. The husband beats her. She leaves. She works at a deli and cleans houses to get her kids an education. She becomes a citizen. She marries an illegal gay immigrant. He pays her for citizenship. Her children grow up, and they get good jobs in the foodservice industry in Vegas and Florida. Now she bides her time at St. Stephen's. She takes four-day weekends often to visit her kids.

As Father explains, "She is a survivor. She transformed herself from an immigrant innocent to a savvy assimilated immigrant. Yes, Ben, she may seem like a lazy Latina housekeeper. But, she is plodding along, making the system work for her. So, please have a little understanding." I feel like I should make the sign of the cross and say an Act of Contrition. That's what you do after Confession.

After, Father Tom arranges for the priests to load the fancy new dishwasher and run it every night. I clear the table, and neither Georgina nor I do the dishes. Georgina does not talk to me for two weeks. Then she warms. And this is how it goes. We have our blowouts. Like when she said I had to use a full pot of water to boil potatoes. "You know they are made of 90% water, so you must fill the pot." I told her that was stupid. After a few weeks, she always thaws.

Around the holidays, we all go to a party at Joyce's house. She has invited parishioners and the church staff to her townhouse in the Village for a Christmas celebration. Her husband supervised the remodeling of MOMA; their townhouse is impeccably decorated. The spread is terrific. Georgina shows up all dolled up; she is not the all-around housekeeper. She looks very Tom Petty, an American girl. And she and everyone else drink like one too. Me, I am an alcoholic, and I don't drink since my 50th birthday. I had a big shebang, and I blacked out after the first hour. I am an alcoholic who cannot stop at 1 or 2 drinks. I drink till I black out. At Joyce's party, the church staff is soused. Georgina takes this opportunity to bond with me further, fueled by hops.

"*Benhamin*, let me tell you about La Malinche. She was an Indian native, traded to the Spanish as a slave. She became their translator. She helped Cortez beat the Aztecs.   She was a victim, collaborator, survivor and is now a hero to us Chicanas. Us *feministas* refer to her as a "mother."   She married Cortez, had children, and was instrumental in the Spanish conquering native Mexico."

I am at first taken aback by the worship of a collaborator. Being Filipino, I take on the colonial slant, a collaborator is a traitor. But Georgina talks like some Latina Gloria Steinham, Betty Friedan, about La Malinche, and I understand and appreciate this kind of heroine.

She is speaking now like a bodega owner on the Upper West Side. She usually talks like my latino waiter friends do. They speak this Spanglish stereotype to customers, a sense of humor reinforcing their speech. They say "Si senor" like Speedy Gonzalez. To customers, they say, "Si senor...but of course, more *cerveza*." It works. They make the best tips.

Georgina speaks like that to priests and parishioners but no longer with me. She drops her guard, and even speaks Spanish. Because of my limited kitchen Spanish, she reverts to English with a slangish gal slant. *"Claro que si, Benhamin."* And then she drops to, "Don't be playing me, Ben, you think you some kinda playah?

———

She calls me *Benhamin* all the time now; I call her Georgy Girl. Her kids are grown and flown. She sleeps with Mexican cooks. They send her free frozen margaritas and free food during Friday Happy Hour. These men take care of her. She takes care of them.

When she finds out I am gay, we attempt gurl talk. She tells me about her gay marriage. She married for the money, she a citizen, he a gay *Hispano*. She likes to talk about her boyfriends. We develop a common thread.

We have a lot of fun assigning nicknames to the priests. Father Barnabas has a beard, so he is known as Barbas for a while. Barbas becomes Barabas. Father Al is from the deep south, even plays banjo, and performs bluegrass. His complexion is so white we call him Father Cloro, as in Clorox. And Father Charles is from the outskirts of London. He always said he trusted no one, a trait leftover from Colonial Britain. That is the stereotype of Londoners. We call him Father Blanco, that is his English last name, Father Charles White.

One lunch, I see her and Carlos, the maintenance man, inside the nearby porn shops. I wave to them, wondering, Georgy Girl has *cojones*, works at a church, and takes a lunch break at a peep show place? Together with Macho Carlos?

Later I ask them why they were in there. Their response, they ask me to get the condoms. Carlos and Georgy Girl say they need lots. I ask them, "What do you need so many for? Never mind."

Carlos is Peruvian, also married with children, all grown up now.

Carlos says, "What we were doing in the porno place last Thursday when you saw us at lunch, we were looking for condoms."

"And they did not have any?"

"*Siii*, they have, they have! *Muy caro*! Too expensive, my friend. And I need the *doble* X size."

Georgy Girl interrupts, " *Benhamin*, me too, I need the doble X size!"

"*'Sus, Marya, Yosep,* " I reply. That's Filipino slang for Jesus, Mary, and Joseph. Latinos get it because it is based on Spanish.

I stop by the Gay Center on 13th Street. It used to be a regular school, then a middle school for troubled gay teens. Now it is The Lesbian, Gay, Bisexual, Transsexual, Questioning, and everything else under the sun Center. Condoms there are handed out free. On my way to work, I grab a bunch, rainbow colors, for my knapsack. Georgina is having coffee in the laundry room. "Look what I have, goodies." There must have been dozens in the knapsack, maybe five dozen. Later that day, Carlos corners me and says, "*Benhamin*, can you give me some more condoms? Georgina, she gives me only 3."

"Carlos, she has at least 30 condoms."

"I know she has a lot. She says she needs them all for her boyfriend's birthday."

"Yeah, right. Is she going to blow them up and decorate her apartment? *Sus, Marya, Yosep!*"

———

One day I come in, and Carlos waylays me. "*Benhamin*, something happened. They sent Georgina home. They had a meeting in the office, two priests with her, Father Blanco and Father Tom. She left, crying, how you say, those crocodile tears. I ask her, 'Georgina, what's wrong?' and she just yelled. 'I cannot talk, Carlos!' She runs to the laundry room with the crocodile crying. I asked Father Tom what happen? He just said she not work here. I asked why, and he says we will not talk about it. But, *Benhamin,* he will talk to you. Find out what happened."

I ask Father in the laundry room. He is showing Gary, his health care guy, around. Gary is the new Gal Friday. Carlos is wrong. Father says, "We will not talk about details. She no longer works for us".

Over the next few days, a picture develops. Father Blanco, he did not trust Georgy Girl. He laid a trap. In the early morning, he always heard mouse noises from the liquor closet, rustling paper. He sets up a security cam in there.

The priests confirm nothing. They say they got her on videocam. Money from the collection baskets. Those big baskets, especially during the holidays. Georgy Girl has had her hand in them all this time! "Gurl," the gay parishioners say when retelling the story. "Stay out of that closet, honey. That will get you nowhere."

Carlos and I joke, "Georgy Girl smart. The priests don't give us a bonus. Go to the closet on Monday. Need to go on vacation, Monday, go to the closet."

She comes in one day to sign papers for severance pay. Says hello to no one. She has worked many years for St. Stephen's, all ten with Father Tom. Another decade with Father Tonio, the previous pastor. The archdiocese pays her a good severance package.

I tell the gay parishioners, "Gurl, nuh uh, it pays to hang out in the closet with the Archdiocese of New York City."

Gregory J. Glanz

Greg has spent a lifetime pursuing creative writing and storytelling. He has a passion for the hidden tale, the ignored subject, the absurd. His publishing credits include short fiction in *The Dark Sire*, *Blood & Bourbon*, and anthologies from *MicroMacroCosm*, *WriteHive*, and *Knight Writing Press*, as well as his book, *In Human Shadow*, recently released by Nordic Press. He is a homebrewer and biking enthusiast. Surprisingly, they go exceedingly well together as more and more microbrews chase thirsty bicyclists across city trails. In his spare time, he loves to travel through the villages of Ireland and document rural, generational Irish pubs in the series, "A Proper Pint" ().

Of Wolverines and Cowards

By Gregory J. Glanz

I remember Mom going off to a "family meeting." I expected big things to come from those clan meetings. Indeed. Looking back, all I see is pain; people in pain, people causing pain, people making pain a way of life, a way to survive. Whenever I faced those truths, my stomach churned and my bowels turned to water. Unlike a wolverine that defecates on the carrion it discards, not wanting anything or anyone to use what they've left behind, there is no pride nor selfishness in me, just shame and cowardice.

Since the reason for the meeting was going to affect the entire family, profoundly, I imagined, only the elders took a spot on the decision-making body. I never, before this, knew why a decision was made or even what made it necessary. But I trusted!

The 'elders' consisted of two drunks, two divorcees (both, at the very least, lushes) and a drudge. Or so it was before the meeting.

My grandfather was one of the drunks, though that didn't matter to my little brother, Arty, nor to me. Grampa would take us to Krueger's Bar after he got off work from the packing plant and buy us root beers until supper was ready. Oh, what a life.

The other drunk, and the purpose for the meeting, I was to find out later, was Uncle Bert. Grandfather never drank with Bert, something which hadn't caught my attention yet. The two divorcees were my mother, Lois, by name, and Aunt Mary. My grandmother was the resigned drudge, unwittingly house-wiving her way down the path to oblivion. Painful.

So Arty and I waited, and we wrestled. In the house! This was not common practice, but being ordered to wait for Mom to finish at the meeting, and being the restless boys we were...

I was short and a little obese. My skin was pale and I carried a rather faltish blob of flesh for a nose. Arty, two years my junior, was only a normal little kid with sandy brown hair and a back full of freckles.

Keeping one ear open for Mom's arrival, we chased each other around the house, picking up whatever implement we found and using it to beat on the other brother. We couldn't run far, though, living on only the second and third floors of the right side of a quadruplex. The 65-year old brown brick (once a crisp red) house was split up into four sections. This sounds like less than splendid living conditions, I'm sure, but keep in mind that the landlady made more money that way and we paid less rent. It wasn't great, but Arty and I, at least, didn't notice the hardship. And we survived.

Eventually, and as always, we ended up wrestling on Mom's double bed, which was not only perfect as a wrestling mat, but was thought of as the only luxury we possessed.

I was about to pin Arty when the front door banged open and my mother's quick footfalls froze me where I was, smothering Arty, while both of us dripped sweat on the sheets.

"What in the hell is going on here?" my mom screamed from underneath a pile of gray-streaked, black hair. Her cat's eye glasses made her look, at that time and now and forever, like a berserk, overgrown rabbit.

"N-nothin', Mom. We was just playing," I stammered.

She grabbed each of us by an arm and alternately pulled and paddled us to the stairway.

"Now get in your room and stay there until I call you for supper!"

Bawling, we went up the stairs and immediately buried our faces in our respective pillows, trying to hide our cowardice from one another.

We recovered quickly in those days, though the two hours until supper seemed an eternity to the two boys staring out the window at our summer playground only half-a-block away.

In whispered tones, we discussed our recent abuse. Then, gradually, we once again became the 12- and 10-year-olds we were, inventing games we would never play again just to occupy the time spent in a bedroom surrounded by faded purple pressed-board.

We giggled through our games with a fierce competitive spirit, and then forgot who won and who got punched in the arm and left bruised.

"Supper!"

With this call all games were forgotten. We scrambled down the stairs, trying to trip each other and be the first to the kitchen. On this occasion, I got there first and, turning quickly, grabbed Arty and whispered, "Ask Mom about the family meeting." I wheeled and trotted to the kitchen, slowing down to a walk half-a-step from the doorway.

Arty didn't quite understand that some things shouldn't be mentioned until first spoken of by Mom. Knowing that, I often urged him to find things out for me. Mom, realizing Arty's age and experience-related shortcomings, was more lenient with him.

"We'll talk about that in due time, young man," she said, peering first at Arty and then at me, just in case I felt any defiance toward her edict.

Two hours in a room on a smothering summer day breeds impatience, and so we were always one step ahead of our actions with our thoughts. Mom set the food on the table, still steaming. On this day, it was liver, peas, and mashed potatoes. With our minds racing out the door to enjoy the summer evening around the Mississippi valley, we grabbed the food and began shoveling it onto our plates.

Smack!

I pulled my stinging hand back.

"Wait until we say Grace!"

So we sat with our hands between our legs until Mom sat down, then folded our hands and bowed our heads.

"Thank you, Lord, for these thy gifts we are about to receive, Amen."

I don't like liver and peas much, never have, most likely never will. So when each dish came around to me, I took a sparse serving and tried to pass them on before Mother intoned, "Take more than that, dear."

I smiled and piled a few more peas on, and I knew not to stop until Mom had given me her contented smile and looked away.

So there I was, with a mound of peas and a heap of liver, salivating and nauseated at the same time. And I knew that I wasn't going to enjoy the summer evening until my plate was clean. I mushed the liver into the potatoes to disguise the taste. It worked just long enough to get the liver down. By then, any protest from my stomach was either academic or, if vehement enough, ended supper, at least for me. But it would also end the day, because I'd have to go bed straightaway and stay there until the next morning.

Once the liver was done, I had to choke down the peas. This should have been easier because milk washed down peas just as easy as water does a pill. The only problem was that my stomach, by this time, knew that those peas were coming and it rebelled as soon as the milk entered my mouth. You can imagine how long it takes to swallow some thirty or forty peas one at a time.

So, invariably, I was the last one to leave the table on 'peas' night, some five or ten minutes after the others were done. And, invariably, Mom would start the dishes while I sat there, degenerating, seemingly oblivious to my plight. After finishing, I went outside grouchy and beat on Arty for a while to make myself feel better. I sometimes wonder what Arty did to make himself feel better.

That evening we came in just after dark. Our mother scowled at us and said, "Go clean up. Then come here; I want to talk to you."

Remembering what was of such importance to us earlier, but had been usurped by the promise of the outdoors, we hurriedly complied. Soon we were fidgeting on the couch, awaiting the clan edict.

"It wasn't really a family meeting I went to today," Mom told us. "It was a trial."

Arty and I sat in stunned silence.

"Your uncle won't be around for about six months," she stated flatly as she handed us a photograph that had been cut from the local newspaper. It showed Uncle Bert with a blood-smeared face, though I couldn't tell where the wound was, being held in custody by three police officers while he thrashed about. He looked like a fatted, sacrificial calf with his bloated, bullet-scarred belly, compliments of a tour in Vietnam, showing prominently through a torn button-down shirt.

This sight awed and sickened me. Both infamous and noteworthy, it made we want to run to the bathroom. I probably would have if I had known at the time that the picture was more than a month old.

"Your uncle," she continued after a pause which, I now believe, was designed to give us a chance to run into the bathroom if we wanted or needed to, "Is in jail for assault and resisting arrest. The other fella wasn't hurt badly, and his escape consisted of staggering down the street for half-a-block before falling on his face and breaking his nose. The picture is of him squirming a bit when the officers took him to the squad car and eventually to the drunk tank." When I think of it now, I don't even hesitate: I head straight to the bathroom.

So our mother told us how violent Uncle Bert had become. She told us that the family had not supported his efforts at avoiding a short, dry, county jail term. She told us that in six months, after he had served his time and had time to brood, he might come back more drunk, more angry, and more violent than ever. But most importantly, she said, after due pause and in very clear terms, a baseball bat would be considered a reasonable and likely weapon in the case of his unhappy, overly-aggressive return.

My god! Hit my own uncle, whom I no doubt respected, if for nothing else tangible in my pre-teen naivete, than for being my elder. I was speechless. I was mindless. All that kept reverberating through my head was, "No, no, no, no, no." An endless procession of denials.

My mother, who collected Aid for Dependent Children, worked four nights a week at a bakery to survive and, I am now convinced, drank vodka whenever feasible, was telling me to hit my uncle with a bat!

"No!" I cried.

My grandfather, whom I supposed, wrongly, to be penniless just like everyone else in the family, and, I knew, drank whatever he could get through his liver, was telling me to hit my uncle with a bat!

"No!" I cried.

My grandmother, who cooked and cleaned her mind into oblivion, was telling me to hit my uncle with a bat!

"No!" I cried.

My aunt, a barmaid, bartender and barfly, who lived above a barroom was telling me to hit my uncle with a bat!

"No!" I cried.

I brooded for the rest of the night. Arty didn't seem so stung by the digression of events. Or so I figured out the next day when, finally leaving the house late morning, I ran into a friend of ours from down the street. Scotty told me how Arty was spreading lies about the violent acts he was sanctioned by the elders to commit on our dastardly uncle, should it become necessary. I felt like going to the bathroom.

Scotty and I hunted Arty down. We found him in the small woods behind the playground, toying with the inhabitants of an anthill.

"What's the big idea?" I shouted, tossing a rock within a few inches of him.

"Whattya mean?"

"Tellin' everyone about Uncle Bert!" I screamed.

"What's the big deal?"

"Whattaya afraid or something?" interrupted Scotty.

"No, I aint't afraid. But it's nobody's business."

"Aww, you are too afraid."

"I am not. Leave me alone."

"You're afraid to hit your drunken uncle with a baseball bat, 'cause you don't want to get hit back. Chicken," Scotty concluded.

"C'mon, Arty. Let's go." I was frustrated and felt like beating on him. But instead I grabbed him and propelled him the first few feet, to which he shrugged and followed, somewhat perplexed.

When we got home, Mom was waiting for us. "Just what in the hell do you boys think you're doing?"

We looked at each other and then at her with blank faces, fear welling up in our throats, creeping into our minds. My bowels rumbled.

"I don't ever want to catch you two telling the neighborhood about our family problems again," she screamed, pausing long enough on each word to slap one of us, emphasizing her point.

"Is that understood? Now get up to your rooms until I call you for lunch."

Arty, who was crying with great wracking sobs, needed no further prompting. I, being on the verge of tears and not convinced as to the legitimacy of her outrage, ran, like a coward, the opposite direction, out the door.

I slowed just long enough to grab a bat from the outer porch, and down the stairs I went. My mother yelled after me, "Get back here you little sombitch or I'll…" The rest was obscured by the pounding in my ears, the battering of my soul, the rumbling of my bowels.

My mother liked to vent her rage on me, but she never put herself out of her own way to do it. Having me put myself in her way was another matter.

Running toward the playground, I had only one thing on my mind, denying my own cowardice.

As I ran, I saw Scotty sitting by the ball field with a bunch of other guys getting ready to play Indian ball, a form of baseball we played when there weren't enough players to field a complete team. In this game, you needn't run the bases, you needn't throw anyone out, and you don't even need to man the right field side of second base. Just hit and catch, hit and catch. Simple.

"Who says I'm afraid," I yelled, focusing on Scotty from halfway across the playground, drawing the attention of nearly everyone around. "If that drunken son-of-a-bitch comes around looking for trouble, I'll wrap this bat around his goddamn skull!"

"Aww, stop braggin', Rudy. You ain't gonna hit him and you know it."

"If you don't think so, then get up," I said closing on Scotty. "Cause I'll use it on you too, big-mouth." An irresistible challenge, I knew. Scotty stood up and I, panting from the run and with tears streaming down my face now, whopped him one in the belly.

"Anybody else," I challenged, sounding more like a crazed animal barking its distress than anything human. It was met by a lot of blank stares, so I turned and ran into the woods, once again hiding my cowardice. Yes, I'll hit him, I thought.

I found out later that only a few of the less-than-dozen kids on the ball field at the time knew of my uncle's anti-social behavior. I'm not sure any of them even cared, even Scotty. It makes me want to go to the bathroom.

So I carried my bat around the woods, beating on various trees and rocks. It was not a time for revelations, merely hatred. I was reeling through the eddying currents of my family's erratic emotional tides. Confusion had given way to rage, I see that now, and rage to hatred. In this case, these were the necessary elements of pain.

I resolved not to return home until after dark. I knew that worrying was a painful pastime for Mother dear. I also knew that if she didn't know where I was, she would worry. I sneered privately – and went to the bathroom.

After hiding my bat in the woods, not wanting to show off my cowardice, I trekked home late that evening. When I got there, grandfather was waiting on the porch, drinking a bottle of whiskey and staring into the sky. Mom told me once that he had developed a habit of staring away from anyone he was about to address. As far as I knew, he had always done that.

I slouched up the stairs with my eyes on him. He didn't even seem to recognize the fact that I was there, but I knew he was about to speak.

"You shouldn't do that to your Mother, Rudy."

I started crying. Looking back, I don't know if it was the unreasonableness of the statement or just the pressure of returning home after being AWOL. I think that now, I would just turn and leave, never to look back.

I didn't do that, however. I did go inside and face my mother. She said that Arty had told her that the incident was his fault, and she claimed the patience and understanding it would have taken to straighten things out at the time. And why didn't I tell her then?

I had, of course, no answer for her, my left cheek still stinging from the memory.

The next six months went by normally enough, as our family goes. There were no changes, nor were there any family meetings.

When Uncle Bert was released from jail, it was done without incident.

The only thing one might think odd was the fact that my mother bought me a baseball bat for Christmas and had me keep it on the inner porch, even though it was winter. It was a beautiful bat, a Louisville Slugger with Willie Mays' autograph on the barrel. I could see myself hitting home runs with it as soon as I opened the package. It never touched one baseball.

One quiet January night, while Arty and I were supposed to be asleep, and I think Arty was, I heard some muffled voices below my window on the street. I looked out to see my mother, getting home from wherever it was she went on her nights off... and a man. My mother pushed the man away and started down the walk to the steps. The man followed.

"No, goddammit," my mother exclaimed throatily.

With this, she turned and hurriedly made her way to the stairs and up them into the house.

The man just stood there. After a minute or so he grunted, rather loudly, and began to make his way toward the steps. It was then that I recognized Uncle Bert.

At this point, I would normally have alerted my mother, but some wrong-headed chivalrous instinct in me had been awakened. Maybe it was the anger, maybe it was the pain, more likely fear and cowardice blinded me. I decided to face this danger for her.

Sneaking down the stairway from our bedrooms, I crept into the hallway and through the kitchen to the inner porch. It was from there that I watched the hooded figure of Uncle Bert finish climbing the outside steps. He stood for a few seconds on the outer porch before pulling a pocket knife to jimmy the door and slowly open it. I cowered farther into the corner, my chivalry now frozen in my watery loins. Slinking back, I nudged a familiar object, my Louisville Slugger.

If ever I have felt the rallying of the cavalry, that was it. Without so much as a thought, I struck!

I don't remember the blows, but I struck him at least twice, I am told. I don't remember my mother calling the ambulance or the police, but she did. I remember only one thing, and that was how I so desperately clung to my bat, refusing to do anything... but hold blindly to my bat.

The man, it turned out, was not my Uncle Bert, but someone who had picked up my mother in a bar and had wanted to go home with her. He suffered a broken shin bone and a cracked skull. The leg would eventually heal, the mind inside the skull would not.

After a short time, enough to morn his death, I imagine, the man's relatives tried to sue us, but I was supported by law and the courts in my action. You see, he was armed, though in fact only, and he had broken and entered unlawfully. He never knew, indeed was rendered incapable of knowing anything from then on, of the court's decision, and he never knew what hit him or why anything or anyone in fact should have done such a thing. I must confess that neither did I know.

I am unaware of how the bat was removed from my grasp. Certainly not by my mother and certainly not with my consent or even while I was conscious, or at least aware. The bat was more akin to me than anyone else had ever been. I saw it only one more time, as evidence in court – a desecration.

Whether it was returned to my mother or not, I don't know.

I think of it now and then, as you might think of a lost lover. Just as you hope, I hope, and just as you know, I know, too.

I think how detached I am now, how it feels as if I might be narrating someone else's story, some part of another's childhood; maybe something told to naughty adults. But fresh memory returns, and I rush to the bathroom, my aloofness shattered like a mirror run into by an enraged wolverine, trying to attack its own image, cut and bleeding, ignorant of the danger until it's too late.

A person with blue hair

Photo credit Scott Merchant

Kevin A. Harris B.A.

Kevin was born in Northern Ireland in 1968, but was brought up in Australia since 1974. After leaving school, Kevin lived on a hippie commune (self-imposed exile) before finding employment as a clerk, labourer, fruit picker, landscaper, tree lopper, radio DJ, filmmaker, actor, roadie/rigger(for international rock bands), music journalist, musician and even gave teaching a go (and what a waste of time that was having to teach teenagers who have no interest in what you're trying to teach. He got good at dodging tables and chairs). He studied in Uni (literature/Media) before receiving a B.A. He received a Diploma in filmmaking in 2015. For a few years Kevin was in a rock-blues-folk band as a guitarist, harmonica player, singer/lyricist and was nominated for an award (which he missed out on, to his disappointment. He still reckons it was rigged). From there, Kevin struggled with his writing before finally in 2013 he got a break and suddenly four stories were published. He writes horror and crime, and Kevin is single, owns his own property, and is damned proud of being an Irish-Australian. His hobbies include writing, photography, bushwalking, driving, reading good books, gardening, traveling, having coffee with his best friend, and looking after his wildlife. He has travelled through NZ, Ireland and for three months throughout Canada and Alaska and wants to go back again. He has recently finished writing a YA novel that is now ready to be published and is currently writing a crime novel set in the 1860s.

Stories published: 2013-Strange Lucky Mysteries- Simon Says (A crime/supernatural) 2013-Strange Lucky Halloween-Darcy O'Malley's Bride.

THE MOTEL AT THE BACK OF BEYOND

An Australian Ghost Story

By,

Kevin A. Harris

Sweeney didn't like the look of the motel that stood among the trees, but he needed somewhere to stay for a few days until the *heat* died down. A faded sign appeared with the peeling words: **THE MOTEL AT THE BACK OF BEYOND 7KM TO THE LEFT**. The sign was hidden behind lantana; ivy climbed along the rusting steel rail while weeds hugged the steel post that was holding the sign up. Something about the way the sign was designed. Something *unnatural* about it, something not quite right as if it was put there for him.

What a fucking dumb thing to think.

He shook his head, thought nothing of it and continued on driving. He found the road with another big sign pointing in the direction of this motel. The road was partially over-grown, pitted with spine-jarring potholes, but he drove on ahead.

He heard the rumble of thunder before he saw the bolt of lightning splintering the sky, then before he knew it, big drops of tear-like water started hitting the windscreen. They got heavier; water was already lapping against the side of the road, like a watery tongue. The wipers slapped at the rain, swishing back and forth in a hypnotic motion, causing Sweeny to hunch forward, peering out at the torrent of rain, watching the sky light up occasionally. Wind whipped up the rain, bending trees over as if playing touch-our-toes, rocking the car side to side but Sweeney kept driving into the eye of the storm. One thing he did notice, the absence of vehicles, including trucks. It was odd, but he didn't give a damn. Less cars the better.

Earlier that day, he and his mate, Ray, held up a bank. Ray didn't survive as the robbery suddenly botched and ended up in the middle of a gunfight, leaving behind a trail of dead people. And yes, he will blame the dead. It was Ray's fuck up. He shouldn't have shot that guard, but enough of that. What's done was done. He needed shelter, somewhere to hide, somewhere tucked away in the bush. Like this motel coming up.

His side ached and a dull pain thudded behind his eyes. *Lack of sleep*, he thought as he struggled to keep the car on the road. He looked at the sportsbag that sat beside him, patted it and grinned. He switched the radio on and received nothing but statics. He thought he heard music coming from the statics, and frowned as he thought he recognised the tune. *Earth Angel.*

"Earth Angel? Shit, haven't heard that song for fuckin' years." It faded in and out before Sweeney snapped it off. Then, emerging from the dark night, at the end of the rutted road, was a block building made as if from Lego. He arrived at the motel and pulled into the car park. His ribs hurt. He was lucky no blood showed, but Christ it hurt.

"Fuck," he mumbled. Against the backdrop of the oncoming storm, the motel didn't look too inviting. It was seedy and run down, with peeling yellow paint looking like the building was shredding its skin. It was made from cinder blocks that were popular in the forties and fifties and the 'space age' design made Sweeney feel sick. He remembered motels like these from when he was a kid and the smell of dried urine and fleas still haunted him, but his mum moved around a lot, staying in trailer parks and seedy motels, picking up different men each night, and always having some bundle of money sitting on the table. His old man was a prick, he remembered. Always slapping his mother and always slapping him until his mother packed their bags and they disappeared onto a Greyhound Bus that took them both to wherever she could find, always on the move, always working either as a diner waitress and/or prostitute. That was when his father found them. That was one part of his life he erased. Deliberately erased from his memory. The Juvenile correction centre, the foster families, they all don't exist, especially after the death of his mother at the hands of his demented father, who died a few years later in gaol by some inmate who had it in for him. Knifed in the neck. Good riddance to shit.

He shook his head and concentrated on his surroundings. It was ugly; very damned ugly. On the painted brickworks were the words **THE MOTEL AT THE BACK OF BEYOND.**

"What a weird name to call your motel," he muttered as he killed the engine. He noticed a car that was parked next to him and saw something about the car that didn't look right. It looked *ancient*, like cars from the forties and fifties with the winged fenders and the sleekness of the paintwork as if it just came off the assembly line. He shook his head and leaned forward to look out of the windscreen. Heavy drops kept exploding on the screen. *Bugger it*, he thought, *how long is this rain gonna continue?*

He observed the rooms that looked out at him. They were dark, except for two rooms where the lights burnt brightly, and he felt as if the rooms were *watching* him. He got out, grabbed the sportsbag, and hurried to the main office through the rain. He pushed open the door and a small bell rang announcing his arrival. He could hear music coming from the room at the back. The same song he heard on the radio coming in. A song he hated. A song with too many sour memories attached.

The foyer had an ancient coke machine, the fifties style, that rattled, an old wooden long desk with a small bell, a rack of post cards sitting on the desk and a corkboard at the back that had keys on hooks. In the foyer, itself, there was a settee that had seen better days. He rang the small bell on the desk and continued to look around. He looked at rack that had a few brochures tucked in the wires. *Have a Holiday, you deserve it.* Weird. Or one of a woman in the swimsuit from the fifties standing, looking over her shoulder, with the words: *Wish You Were Here.* Something wasn't right with this. Like as if he just stepped into an episode of *Happy Days*. He was half expecting Richie Cunningham and Ralph Malph and that half wit Potsie coming in, followed by canned laughter and Fonzie saying *heyyy* with both thumbs up and the collar of his jacket turned up.

Childhood memories of sitting in front of a black and white TV watching Get Smart *and* Happy Days *while his mother 'entertained' some of the 'gentlemen' she picked up at the local bar drifted into his mind, and he remembered hearing the grunts and groans coming from the bedroom, then the 'gentleman' would come out, zipping his pants up and disappear out the door. His mum used to come out and light a cigarette up and sit, waiting for the next one to arrive, looking worn out. Sometimes she would hum* Earth Angel. *Most times she was sporting a bruise and...*

Someone cleared their throat behind him. He turned around and saw a small man with a pockmarked face. His hair was done like the hairstyle from the fifties- a ducktail and greased back. When he smiled, he flashed rotting teeth. He wore a loud coloured shirt like the ones they used to wear back in the fifties, something a dero wouldn't be caught dead in. Sweeney had to stifle a giggle. *Mate, you look like a right fuckin wombat in that shirt. Deadset, mate, a right fuckin wombat*, he wanted to say. The bloke looked up at him, leaning on the desk.

"Help yah?" He asked, some of his words whistled through the gap in his front teeth. "Lookin' for a room, huh?"

"Good guess," Sweeney said with a grin. "But only for a few nights, eh?"

"Huh uh, that's what they all say, mate," the pock faced man pushed over a ledger, reached behind, and grabbed a set of keys and sat them on the desk. "Name..." He looked at Sweeney. "Most people just write an alias. I don't tell."

Sweeney looked at the guy with knitted brows. He said nothing and wrote only his surname then looked up and pushed it across to the bloke. "Now you know my name, what's yours? And don't say Elvis or Buddy or I swear to God, I'll deck ya."

"I've many names," he said without sounding put out as he tossed the keys at Sweeney. "Yer room eight. Straight down the corridor. Won't miss it."

"What people normally call you?" Sweeney insisted asking. Just to goad the guy.

"Whatever," the man answered, then turned and went back into the back room. Sweeney could hear the song had been turned up louder. "*Ohhhh...ohh....ohh....ohh....Earth Angel, Earth Angel, will you be mineeeee?*"

Sweeney left the office and stood outside, listening to the rain bashing the roof. He sighed and walked up the cold corridor, rain lashing at his feet. He walked past one of the rooms when he heard what sounded like someone weeping, a woman weeping, from inside. He stopped, wondering whether he should do something, then decided that it wasn't his affair, so he continued wandering until he found the room.

The room wasn't much. Floral wallpaper decorated the walls, a radio sitting on a shelf but there was no TV, he noticed, and the bed was a single bed that was tucked up against the window. A door led into the bathroom that had a bath, a toilet, and a sink. No towels. He went back and threw the bag on the bed. He switched the radio on, and that annoying song was on, *Earth Angel*.

"What the fuck is it with this song?" He switched it off. "You gotta be kidding me. Bleedin hell, is this all the entertainment I'm gonna get? The fuckin' song over and over? Man, this is *my* version of Hell...should be glad, though, could be worse. Could be *Popcorn*."

He lay down on the bed and thought about what the last few days just held. He robbed a bank and took over $170,000 in cash, which wasn't much. One thing that played on his mind, the gunfight he had with one of the guards, the stupid prick. He knew he shot him dead, but before the bastard died, he shot back at him, grazing him. He lifted up his shirt and saw a red mark across his ribs. It ached but not badly. He pulled the shirt down and saw no blood on the shirt, but didn't that bullet penetrate his shirt? He frowned but shook his head. Nah, missed me by a country mile. Pity about Ray though. Poor bastard, I'll spend your half wisely, Ray me old China plate. The other guard shot Ray in the throat but Ray got off one hell of a lucky shot, and killed the guard with a bullet between the poor man's eyes before both men fell to floor dead. Sweeney fled with the sports bag as the alarm was triggered and here he was. Alive.

He smiled and picked the sportsbag up. He unzipped it and peered in. The money smiled back at him before he zipped it closed again. He placed the bag at the bottom of the bed and placed his hands behind his head. He closed his eyes when he heard weeping coming from the room next to his. It was that woman again. He slid off the bed and walked to the door, opened it, and stepped out into the wet night. The weeping stopped only to be replaced by that song again.

"*Earth Angel, Earth Angel, will you be mine?*" He frowned and was about to step inside when the door to the room next to him opened and a pretty young woman who looked in to be in her late teens, early twenties, stepped out. She wore a dress and a cardigan that looked like it came from the fifties. It looked like as if she just stepped out of *Grease*. Her hair was blond and tied back in a ponytail. When she swayed, he caught a glimpse of the lacy hem of her petticoat.

Since when did chicks started wearing petticoats? He thought, then shook his head.

She didn't see Sweeney standing there at first as she took out a cigarette pack, shook out one and lit it. She blew out smoke when she saw Sweeney standing there. She smiled.

"Hello," she said with a smile. She was attractive and was wearing very little make up. But there was something not right about her. But what was it?

"G'day," he replied as he stepped out of the doorway. The rain was still tumbling down. "Pretty heavy rain."

"Always raining here," she said, blowing smoke out. Sweeney wasn't sure if he heard that correctly. Before he could say anything, the girl started humming *Earth Angel* and swayed as she hummed. She stopped and looked at Sweeney. "You here for long?"

"Only a few days," he answered. "You?"

"Same. Oh," she held out her hand. "I'm Candy.'

Sweeney took it. "Sweeney."

"That's your first name or last name?"

"Could be either," he grinned. "Candice, am I right?"

She shook her head. "Not really. Just a name I adopted."

"Oh? What's your real name?"

She looked at Sweeney with a strange look in her eyes. "You know, I've forgotten. You believe that? I've been using Candy for so long that I've actually forgotten what's my *real* name is." *Weird*, he thought. *Fancy forgetting your real name.* She smiled and looked at the cigarette pack. "You want one?"

"I don't normally smoke but, what the hell," he took one and saw the name of the cigarette. *Fatima.* "Wow, Fatima, thought that company closed down in the '60s?" She looked at him as if he was mad and giggled. "You're funny."

Before he could reply, that song started again. She started to sway to it. "What is it with that song? Keep hearing it since I've arrived."

She looked at him, bemused. "Don't you like it?"

"Not if it's been played so many times."

"Then don't listen to it then," she snapped, giving Sweeny a jolt. Fair enough, he thought, shouldn't have said what I said. But he did find it odd. The cigarettes from a company that went broke nearly fifty years ago, the song from the fifties, even the way she and the hotel owner were dressed, it was as if he had just walked into a fancy dress party or...*The Twilight Zone.*

"Sorry, it's been a long day for me and I'm...well...tired, I suppose," he smiled, but she said nothing, stepped on the cigarette, and without saying bye, she went back into her room leaving Sweeney out on his own, shocked. He stared at the door, then when he turned, he saw the owner watching him. The pockmarked faced man turned his back and disappeared inside. Sweeney grounded the cigarette and also disappeared inside, feeling bemused.

During the night Sweeney woke up.

The rain was hammering against the roof... what was it that Candy said? *"Always raining here."* That bugged him, but it wasn't the rain that woke him but both the weeping and that damned bloody song. He wondered if he should check up on Candy, see if she was okay and maybe ask that pock face bloke to turn the fucking music off. What is it with that bloody song anyway? Beginning to get on his nerves. Like being in a mental ward. He slipped out of bed and went to the door, opened it, and peered out.

"What are you looking at?" Asked a voice from the darkness, scaring the hell out of Sweeney. A fat man stepped out of the darkness wearing a white shirt, dark tie, and dark pants that were held up by braces. He was smoking a cigarette and drinking from a flask. His face looked like the face of a bulldog with heavy jowls. "You're that bloke who arrived earlier on. I saw you talking to Candice earlier."

"Just been friendly," protested Sweeney, not knowing why he was protesting.

"Yea, fair enough," the fat bloke said as he drank from the flask then offered Sweeney some. Sweeney accepted and drank. It was whiskey. He handed the flask back to the fat bloke who took another hit from it before putting the cap back on. He watched the rain, then looked back at Sweeney. "Here long?"

Second time tonight he was asked that question. "No, here for a night or two."

"They all say that," echoing what the pock marked face man said earlier on. He drew another long sip on the flask, "I've been here for a while. So has she.'

"Is she okay? I heard her weeping."

"Yeah, yeah, she's fine," he took the cap off his flask again, took a long hit on it before passing it to Sweeney. Sweeney accepted. "What's your name, mate? I'm Morgan."

Sweeney handed the flask back. "Sweeney."

Morgan nodded. They said nothing but watched the rain tumble. Then the song floated through the air. Morgan had his eyes closed, listening, silently mouthing the words.

"What is it with that song?' Sweeney had to ask…again. Morgan opened his eyes and looked at Sweeney with his eyes half-mast. "I mean, that's the, I don't know, third, fourth time I heard it tonight."

"Well, we happened to like it," he said, voice sounding like a growl. They sure are touchy about this song, Sweeney thought. Mind you, I'm the same with AC/DC and the Stones but not *this* touchy. The fat man continued staring at him. "You obviously don't like the song, do yah?"

"Aren't you sick of it playing over and over?" Sweeney asked, ignoring Morgan's question.

"No," he growled, snatching the flask out of Sweeney's hands, and disappearing into his room, slamming the door. Sweeney stood there, shook his head.

"Fuck, speaking about being fussy over a fucking song but this is ridiculous," he muttered before going back into his room. He lay on the bed, staring at the ceiling, remembering the events of the day before shifting off to sleep. Back to his childhood of unwanted memories. Ones he locked up in a cage but now had broken free…*Earth Angel, Earth Angel…*

The next morning, the rain was still lashing against the window, but Sweeney was getting anxious, wanting to leave just in case the police arrived, for some reason. He checked the sports bag again, made sure the money was there before re-zipping. His mind kept replaying the scene inside the bank: Ray getting shot with a hole in his throat, the guard falling back with a hole between his eyes as the other one shot back at Sweeney before he fled to the car and drove off like a bat out of hell, but it seemed like a dream, a weird dream to be precise. He remembered feeling that bullet grazing (or did it graze him?), the burning sensation. He must have blacked out somewhere along the way because all he remembered was seeing that sign pointing to this motel.

He got off the bed and stood looking at the rain. "Bugger," he muttered softly. He sighed and walked back out and saw Candy standing, looking out at the rain. *Earth Angel* was playing, and Candy was swaying to the music. He walked over and stood next to her. She had her eyes closed and was mouthing the words. Sweeney noticed that she wore the same clothes that she had on yesterday. She opened her eyes and saw Sweeney, smiled at him.

"I remember the first day I arrived here," she softly said. "Just had a fight with my boyfriend and ran away from the creep. It was a Sunday, and it was wet. I must've ran for *hours* because I somehow ended up here and been here ever since."

"How long has that been?" Sweeney asked.

She smiled, took out a cigarette, offered Sweeney one. He took it and offered her a light. She blew the smoke out at the rain. She stared out blankly. Sweeney frowned as he saw her hair was matted with blood as if she had a head wound. He was going to say something but she suddenly changed the subject. "I used to be a movie actress."

"Oh? What movies were you in?" Curiosity overtook him, still fascinated by the blood in her hair. *How the fuck did she come with that head wound?*

"Nothing fancy. I once acted with James Dean, though. Wasn't that long ago. Before I came here. He's a lovely man, Jimmy is, though wouldn't keep his hands to himself. He got a movie coming out soon."

Sweeney frowned. "I thought he was dead?"

She stared at him and giggled, "He's still alive and kicking, you silly goose."

"Oh," he shook his head. Was this chick an escaped psycho or had that head wound *really* fucked her up? He was *convinced* that James Dean was dead. Just play along with it. Must be a halfway house for recently discharged mental patients, Sweeney thought and grinned. "Oh, okay and, um, what movie was that?"

"It was a stage play to be honest. I kissed him," she blew more smoke out then her face darkened with anger. "My boyfriend, he's a very jealous man. Doesn't like me doing things. Wants me to be tied to the kitchen sink and drop a litter of brats. Bastard," she hissed. "Rotten bastard. He won't find me here. I'm sure of it."

"Oh," he said again, not knowing what else to say. He looked around before looking at her again. There was something not quite right with this girl. To be honest, there was something not quite right with *this place.* Then that bloody song came back on.

"*Earth Angel, Earth Angel, will you be mineeeee?*" Cooed the girl, gently rocking as if she was in a trance. Sweeney was convinced that she was madder than a cut snake. Her clothes were outdated; the cigarettes she smoked were really outdated. She even thought that James Dean was still alive and kicking when he kicked the bucket in '55. And that song, it's older than Moses himself. Something was wrong with this picture. He felt he was in the *Twilight Zone* or something. Stuck out here in this redneck *Deliverance* cow-cocky motel with a bunch of fucking lunatics. He needed to piss off and piss off ASAP, take his chances with the pigs. But the trouble was the rain. It hadn't stopped pissing down and it wasn't causing any flooding, just really teeming down. No thunder. No lightning. Not like last night, just teeming rain. It was getting too much for Sweeney.

"This rain," he finally said, breaking the silence. 'Is it ever going to ease off?"

She laughed. "No."

"No?" He asked, incredulously.

"No, it always rains here. But don't you love the smell of it? How fresh it is?"

She was mad, had to be. He said nothing and grounded the remains of the cigarette, then left her to her humming. He walked down to the main office and entered. The man with the Elvis quiff, was chewing on a toothpick, reading *Screen Annual* with Ava Gardener on the front cover. He looked up and saw Sweeney standing there, then smiled.

"I see Ava Gardener is marrying Frank Sinatra. Man, Nancy's going to be pissed off. Hope it's better than the marriage between her and that midget, Rooney."

"They got divorced," said Sweeney. "But never mind, mate, Nance will end up rootin old Ronnie 'Raygun' Reagan and he'll become Prez of America."

The man stared at him then smiled as he put the magazine down. "Now, what can I do for you?"

"I wanna use your phone," Sweeney said.

The man shook his head and laughed. "Ain't got one."

"What? You haven't a phone?"

"Don't see the need for them."

"You're kidding me?"

"Nah."

Sweeney shook his head. "I would like to get away from here."

"Oh, we all do. Morgan and Candy wants to get away from here. Even me. But, my dear friend, we just can't. Including you, we're all here. Stuck."

"What? This is pure madness. Where's your fucking telephone?" He demanded, spittle running down his chin. Sweeney viciously swiped at it.

"Just told ya, ain't got one. No need, either." Sweeney stared at the man.

"What's going on here?' Shouted Sweeney, spittle flying everywhere then grabbed the owner by the shirt, dragging him halfway over the counter, knocking things over. The man just smiled, but Sweeney roared, "Fuckin' tell me, cunt!"

The man shook his head, "Surprised that you haven't caught on. Everyone are dead." Did he just hear him right? *Everyone here are dead?* "Poor Candy, yeah, she was killed while walking along the side of the road. She was trying to get away from her boyfriend when she was hit by a car that didn't stop. She was dead. Morgan, well, he was drunk when he'd plowed over a cliff after clipping a girl on the side of the road-"

"Whoa, hold on there," Sweeney said disbelievingly, "I'm not quite catching what you're saying. Candy, the girl who I shared a cigarette with, was...what? Killed by that fat bloke, uh...Morgan...who plowed over a cliff? And they all ended up here?"

"Yeah," he said, in a matter-of-fact tone. "Everyone who arrives here are simply *dead*," he smiled. "This is a motel for the dead, a rest place kinda thing before moving on, a personal hell perhaps? Candy's sin was she was an actress and her boyfriend hated that and thought she was seeing men on the side, which she wasn't.

Morgan had a problem with both cocaine and booze. The afternoon of his death, he had several rails of coke and several shots of tequila and rum. He could barely see when he drove down the road. He hit some girl who was wandering along the road and...went over," he demonstrated a car going over the cliff. "Kaboom."

"No fucking way," Sweeney shouted. "You're off your bloody rocker. How can that be possible? What about me?"

"Ah," he smiled. "Yes. You're an interesting case. You were shot by the bank guard."

"No, I bloody wasn't. No one shot me."

"Think again, Todd."

"How do you know my name?" He said, stepping back.

"Mate, I know fucking everything. It's my duty to. Look, you saw that red mark on your ribs, yeah?" Sweeney nodded. "That's where the bullet got you. You died on the way here. Your car crashed, but you were already dead."

"But..."

"Face it, Todd, you're dead and you're a *ghost*," smiled the man, then he picked his magazine up again. "You mind? I want to keep reading about Ava and Frank," and went back to reading. Sweeney walked out and stood there, then sighed. He walked to his car, opened the door, and got in. He tried starting the engine, but nothing happened. He sat there before banging the steering wheel with his fist then got out and went to his room, sat down and wept.

"I'm dead," he moaned. "Fucking dead. God, why, why me?" He stared at the sports bag and kicked it off the bed. "Fuck it. Fuck it all to hell!"

He sighed and got up and looked out at the tumbling rain and started humming *Earth Angel*.

There's a ruin of a motel out in the bush but no one knew about it, nor cared. The bush took it over but the ghosts of the people who live there still do their everyday thing: listening to the Penguins sing *Earth Angel*, reliving past dreams. It's the motel where time stands still. Be careful, you never know, you might be the new occupant in one of the rooms in the Motel At The Back of Beyond.

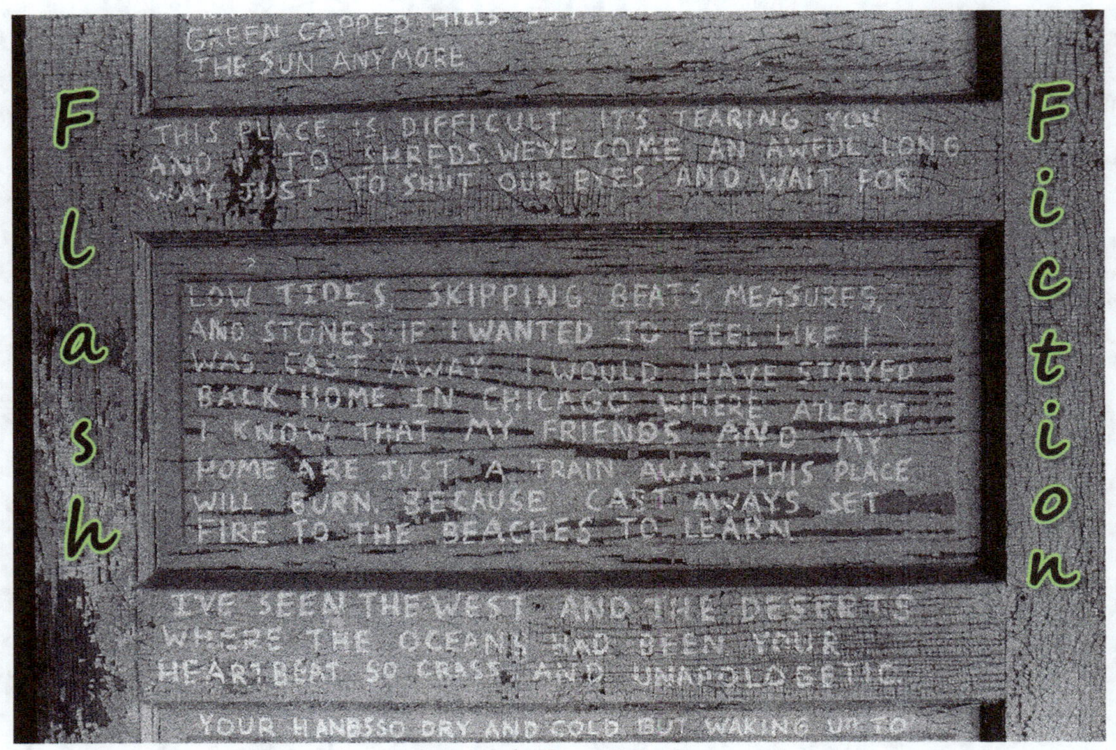

Image by George L Stein

Sleeping

By

Jodie Baeyens

"Hey, girls. I'm home." Jamie tossed her purse on the table next to the front door and dropped her keys in the green bowl on the same table. She could hear the sound of *The Little Mermaid* playing in the living room.

"You don't even come greet your dear old mom anymore," she asked to the silence. An uneasy feeling came over her that she shook off.

"I brought home Happy Meals for dinner," she said as she started unloading the food from the bag and placing everything in the right spots. Caroline had to have apple slices and Madeline would be furious if her extra fries were in her sister's seat. The toys got set aside until after dinner or no one would eat.

"Come on, the food is getting cold," she called walking into the living room. The credits of the movie were playing. Normally Madeline would have restarted the movie by now. As Jamie got closer to the couch, she saw that the two girls' heads were touching and they looked like they were sleeping. Jamie picked up a blanket and walked around the couch to place it over them.

They weren't sleeping.

Jamie screamed and dropped the blanket. In the years to come, she would never remember another moment from that night or how she ended up in the jail cell.

Hands

By

Amy Fenster

Her hands had been beautiful. Long, slender fingers, covered by smooth supple skin. Nails always manicured, but never polished. She felt that the color of nail polish detracted from the natural beauty her hands possessed. People had always admired them, and she had always been rather proud of them. She wore cotton gloves to bed to protect them and moisturized three times daily with milk and honey. Now as she examined the hands that had been a source of so much pride, even vanity, she admitted, an overwhelming sense of melancholy settled over her. Hers were no longer the hands of a young woman. Time had stolen everything from her. The hands were still beautiful, despite age, but they served as a constant reminder of all she'd worked for and all she had lost. These were the hands that had tenderly caressed the face of a young lover, lost to war. These hands had created watercolors and oil paintings equal in skill and content to any of the masters. They had tended to injured soldiers and given comfort to the sick, many of whom passed from life, while still within her grasp. These hands had gently stroked the hair of peacefully sleeping babies. These hands had then been suffered to bury the same babies. One hand had worn the ring of a man she knew was her soulmate. These hands had clung to him, but failed to hold him there.

Fin

Trigger Warning

VOL #2

Magazine

Trigger Warning Magazine

Issue 2

Copyright © 2025 Trigger Warning Magazine

Authors retain all rights to their work

Consider Yourself Warned

There is a time and a place for trigger warnings. Art isn't one of them. Art is meant to evoke emotion. It shouldn't be shocking for the sake of shock or offense, but it should not be censored. If an artist must give a content or trigger warning before a person reads or experiences the art, the power of the piece is often diminished.

By opening this magazine, you consent to being triggered. You consent to being exposed to art that you might not like or that makes you feel something you weren't expecting or didn't want to feel. Art is about making people feel.

There will be no trigger warnings here.

You will experience the art as it was meant to be read and seen.

Our sincere hope is that at least one piece in this magazine elicits an emotion in you that you didn't expect.

If you don't like what you see, go to our submissions page, and show us what you got.

About the editors

Poetry Editor - Jodie Baeyens

Jodie Baeyens is a mother/bonus mother, poet and teaches to support her writing habit. When she isn't trying to find the pen she was just holding, she can be found in the forest dancing beneath the full moon. Originally hailing from New York, she now considers herself a citizen of the world because she has never settled into one place. Her poetry has recently been featured in *Door is a Jar* and in *Peregrine's Fall Journal*. Her forthcoming Chapbook, *Conversations We Never Had*, was the Winner of the 2022 Vibrant Poet Award. Follow her writing at or on Facebook at . '

Fiction Editor - Amy Fenster

Amy Fenster is a novelist, screenwriter, coffee enthusiast and wrangler of small children. She has a Master's degree in creative writing and uses it to subdue unruly characters. Amy began writing at the age of three and has written several screenplays and novels. She writes women's fiction, which is a fancy way to say she does not stick to one genre, but her focus is always to create strong female characters. Amy grew up in New York, but now lives in a paradisiacal land known as San Diego, California. Her hobbies include playing Barbies, Wiccan rituals, keeping small children and animals alive, lots of coffee and trying to stay up past 10:00 PM.

Art Editor - George L Stein

George L Stein is a New Jersey photographer shooting in the art, urban and rural decay, street, alt/portrait, and surreal genres. He has been previously published in Tofu Ink Arts, Sunspot Lit, Wrongdoing Magazine, and Fatal Flaw, among others. Online: insta @steincapitalmgmt, @georgelstein and @darkmuse, as well as . All uncredited art is property of George L Stein.

A person with wings holding a tombstone by George L Stein

BABY BOY

By Robert Tustin

The old churchyard is still here although the church has long since fallen into disrepair. It's little more now than a steeple toppled over.

The villagers nearby carted off all the good timber. The local blacksmith,it's said, reclaimed the bronze bell he'd donated in better times before the long winters.

They still speak of that big bronze bell he so painstakingly sweated over, and which rang out so clearly amongst the tall pines in the neighboring dell.

The carefully placed stones in the churchyard yet stand to mark the graves but the names and epitaphs have, to slow time, begun to fade away except for the one marked BABY BOY.

That stone still reads deep and clear as the day the mason chiseled it there.

The moss hugs that stone and the ivy anxiously climbs it as if to say-- "BABY BOY, let's play."

I like to come here late September and pray to the indifferent winds of fate. I say. "Scatter soon you fickle winds all the leaves and let them like a mobile in the air swirl just for him as he lay here."

Hanging On

By Robert Tustin

I've become a ghost--A walking shadow

Of my former self

Haunting unfrequented courtyards

With tricking fountains.

I'm the lonely idler on that stool

Sits at the end of the long

Bend in each local bar where years from now, when I am gone,

And the bar has changed hands

Several times they won't let anybody

Sit at because of...that guy...

Used to sit there...

whose name

Escapes them though they know

He always had a pilsner close at hand

As well as a pen and a notebook

To record the little unremarkable

Goings on of those yet living.

And every now and then a patron

Will point and swear

They saw a guy right there

Just there for a split second

At the abandoned stool

Sits at the bend in the bar

Sipping a tall pale beer

Or else scribbling away...

Aubade

By Robert Tustin

The room looks as if it's been ransacked

And yet smells of sweat, sex

And the sweet scent of her lavender perfume.

The night before had left them both in ruins,

But now the sun is threatening to peek

In at them through the blinds.

She grunts.

He says, "Hello, old friend."

"No," she coos,"Coffee."

"But love, the sun has come

To see your beauty. He's heard your hair

Outshines his golden rays.

Old friend, it does!

And I am greedy. I keep her here with me.

You will have to wait for her beauty, outside,

You who shine down in the morning wood.

I for my part can only raise one ivory column

In salute to this goddess, who even

With her back to me inspires me to such heights.

If I could do more,

O sun, the temple I'd build

Then dedicate to her would be your pleasure

To behold and what you would look forward to

In rising each morning, as I do here."

A person lying on a pillow

"All of Europe Went Into the Making of Me"

by Robert Tustin

"Your English muffin has never had a sunburn in her life."

"I am also Greek and Italian."

"I'm super fair

In the winter but turn a golden brown

In the summer."

O I know my sweet

I have seen the full report and I have dreamt

About it since the day I saw it.

Your England and Wales get so wet,

I don't think I could stand it. My fingers

Would take a walking tour and find those

Dark secret places where true pleasure

Hides, just waiting to be discovered. Mine would

Be a proper and a thorough tour. I would come to learn

The topography of that entire thirty one percent of you.

Then off to your mountains and lush vineyards

Of Italy. The weather is perfect here. You are

So warm for me and your kisses taste like

Red wine as I get drunk on them enough

To make me blush. It may be twenty six

Percent of you but it has absolutely

Taken all of me.

And I absolutely get lost amongst

Your Germanic landscape with its long rivers

And old castles and dilapidated cathedrals

That dot that endlessly rolling and lush fatherland

Just waiting to be discovered by me. You have

A deep and varied history. I would learn it,If you'd let me. I would be the daring duke

Of this fifteen percent of your demesne.

I have always wanted to go to Greece

And though you own only nine percent

It is way too much for me and my

Imagination gets carried away. Here is

Your mountain where you muse it over me.

There are satyrs and nymphs enough here

To sing and dance the night away for us,

But most of all a laurel tree where you gather

The green leaves to gild and make a crown for me.

When I look at you I always seem to see

That seven and that one percent Scandinavian.

Your gorgeously flowing blonde hair in the sun

And your blue-green eyes that sternly yet

Lovingly stare at me to see my flaws but to love

Them and never judge them. Your eyes pierce

Deep to see the battle scars made by former lovers

But also scan the surface because they like

To view the scars acquired by rough and tumble men. I long to be one worthy of your Valhalla.

Your Russia and your Caucuses are cold. This six and four percent of you must be

Where you hide past pain. I will brave it if only to warm

That part of you and show you how worthy

Of love I know you are. I build my fire here

High in the mountains and whisper my soothing

Words to the cold winds gathered there. I tell them

Don't worry. Your long-lost lover has returned again.

Vesper

Anonymous

"You want some sort of fairytale that doesn't exist.
A devotion I don't believe is real," I tell her
as she sits on her side of the bed crying and spinning her
diamond ring around her left-hand finger.
The following day she shows me the next
issue of the magazine she is editing. We flip through the poems
and pause at one.
A classic ode to a lover lying in bed.
Her golden hair against the pillow. The scent of lavender
on her throat. Curves that stop this lover
in his tracks and makes him yell at the sun to beg
for a few moments longer next to her.
"You don't think a love like this exists? This
isn't a love I should expect?"
I laugh and ask if she thinks these two people
are still together. How, I ask,
do you think they ended up? Are they still in that bed somewhere?
She looks at me for a moment and looks away
as she replies. "I think," she sighs softly, "that he still loves her.
Maybe decades later."
"I think that she was never sure if she could trust
a love like that. That she worried if perhaps he only loved
the idea of her. And if he ever really had her,
she would have to find out it wasn't real."
"She may have been young and scared
of the intensity of it all."
I look at the details of the poem again.
The hair I push out of my beard each night.
The smell that lingers on my pillow.
The curves of the body that curls against me as I sleep.
"Maybe," she continues, though I'm not sure I want her to,
"maybe when she left him, she broke him so badly
he could never truly forgive her. Yet still, he kept writing,
about how her hair felt cool in his hands,
about how her skin tasted like vanilla on his lips."
"Maybe, he never stopped loving her. Or maybe,
one day he did. Maybe after 2 or 3 decades,

he finally tried to move on." "But still, even if he finally gave up
one day, decades of believing, of not giving up,
even if he finally did, that seems, to me,
like devotion."
I want to ask her if she still loves him, but I don't.
The look in her eyes tells the rest of the story.
He spent a lifetime devoted to her.
She sits on the bed, spinning
the diamond on her left hand,
wondering.

"Flashlights"

By Adiba Nelson

Once upon a time I wrote poetry

Love poems to be exact

Love poems that were more like

Beacons

Flashlights

Floodlights

Searching for something that might have felt familiar

But familiar to whom?

To me?

How can one search for what one does not have...

What one does not know...

What one has never met...

How could one possibly know what to look for?

Once upon a time I wrote poetry

Love poems to be exact

Waxing on about all the things I would do if I had love

Professing to all the ears in the room

That my love was the best love

The holy love

The healing love

The only love

But how did I know when I hadn't even experienced it?

Other love?

Your love?

My own love?

Once upon a time I wrote poetry

Love poems to be exact

Untitled

By Adiba Nelson

To the baby me that turned her face to the sun and dared not cry in the face of death

To the kindergarten me who understood the meaning of the words "don't tell your mother"

To the junior high me who ran home daily but wasn't a track star

To the high school me who muttered the only words she could think of in the last moments of life

To the college me who didn't know who she was but was looking and searching and begging for love so she wrote poetry

Love poems to be exact

But I don't write poetry anymore

I haven't written a love poem in ages

I haven't needed to

I turned the corner

And there I was

And there you were

And here we are

Like two flashlights

Let's turn them off

and just

Be.

A blurry image of a city by George L Stein

Untitled

By Adiba Nelson

I already know that I will not go to your funeral

I will not climb the church steps

I will not sit on the front pew

I will not come to the mic and stare out at the crowd from behind dark sunglasses and wax

poetic about the life you led, the things you believed and the dreams you had

I will not sit next to your urn and greet the line of ppl gathering to hug me and tell me how

much they loved you and how much you loved me

I will not bring you into my home

I will not set you on the mantle

I will not plant you in the ground with wildflower seeds so I can lament you in spring and watch

you die again in summer

To do even one of these things

Just one of these things

Would kill me too

It would shuttle me to a place I do not know and it is unlikely I'd be able to find my way home

And despite what God might believe, I am not ready to go

I am not ready to be with you there

I wanted to be with you here

So no, I will not go to your funeral

And in this way

We both get to stay

A person wearing a black robe with a skull and tentacles

Artist Cierra Des Os, The Bee Series

The Edge is Closer Than You Think

By Eve Lyons*after ani difranco*

A graffiti of a person's mouth

So many people

talk about

late-stage capitalism

as if this is the end

of something

not the status quo

we've always known

the women in the middle are learning

what poor women have always known

the edge is closer than you think

when your men bring the guns home

Ten black people in Buffalo

lynched while buying groceries,

Twenty-one brown children in Uvalde

killed while in school,

Eight Asian women in Atlanta

from three different parlors.

If we really believed

all lives mattered...

No. Just no.

The salt marsh is dry today

The hummingbirds don't mind

The tide comes in,

The tide goes out

The ocean is rising 3.3 milliliters each year

If we can't care about each other

How can we care about this?

A close-up of a graffiti

I LIVED THE LIFE OF A CHILD INSIDE

By John Tustin

I lived the life of a child inside

who wished to rise from the earth

in a balloon, in a basket

rising to the sky fist upward

to emerge grinningly

above the streets dirty with

apathetic squalor,

the adults meandering unaware

and the other children laughing

the derisive laugh of the afflicted

of the fearful of the broken

at the lone child imagining

he was not more or less than them,

only different than them,

pretending he rose ever higher

and floated always further away

as the other children laughed

and pointed at his feet

which were of course

firmly fastened

to the ground

spiked dead center

by foot long

bloodied nails.

A LITTLE BANG

By John Tustin

It explodes in my head

like cymbals that clash to lead the parade

or the backfire of a Model T.

It's a Little Bang

and it creates a fertile land inside of me –

a tiny land of fruit trees and animals.

I have something

– I have ONE thing –

to completely say,

so I speak in my gibberish, so I wave my hands;

learn flag signaling, Latin, sign language,

the bellowing of whales,

the speaking eyes of old lovers

to say just one thing –

to say one important thing

in very few words

so that you will remember it.

My stomach is empty

but my head is full

and I barf out these very few words

about love or God or children or life

or other things that do not last.

I hold them out to you

in a tin gleam of grandiloquent gobbledygook;

in their small saliva-coated ball with a candy shell

made easy to swallow

so that you will chew on them a moment

and digest one important thing I mean to convey

and please, please

may you always remember it.

Kendra Matott

TANGLED VINES

By John Tustin

She referred to her pubic hair

as Tangled Vines

and joked that men could not help

but become ensnared in them.

That was the word she used:

Ensnared.

She did not say caught or trapped

or entangled.

Damned if she wasn't right.

She always had at least one man in her bed,

one man writing her love letters from afar

and a third squirming on the hook,

waiting his turn.

I haven't even mentioned the ex-husband

who was always lurking in the background.

If I had spoken to her back when I was drinking

or maybe early in the mornings before I had my first

cup of coffee,

she could have ensnared me, too.

Maybe she never tried

but she never seemed to be trying

with any of the others.

She was pretty enough

and didn't seem to age

the way most of us had

but as much as I enjoyed talking to her

and being around her

I never wanted to get down

into those Tangled Vines

and go all Lewis and Clark.

This poem, of course, contains numerous lies –

all poems have at least one.

Everything is true that I've written,

except that I was indeed ensnared myself –

of course I was.

You probably already knew that.

I became ensnared in her Tangled Vines

and lived there

as if I was a living scent

and it's been a long time

since I was stuck in there

but, you know, I'm still in there,

kind of.

In dispirited spirit,

tangled up in her

and all her terrifying goodness.

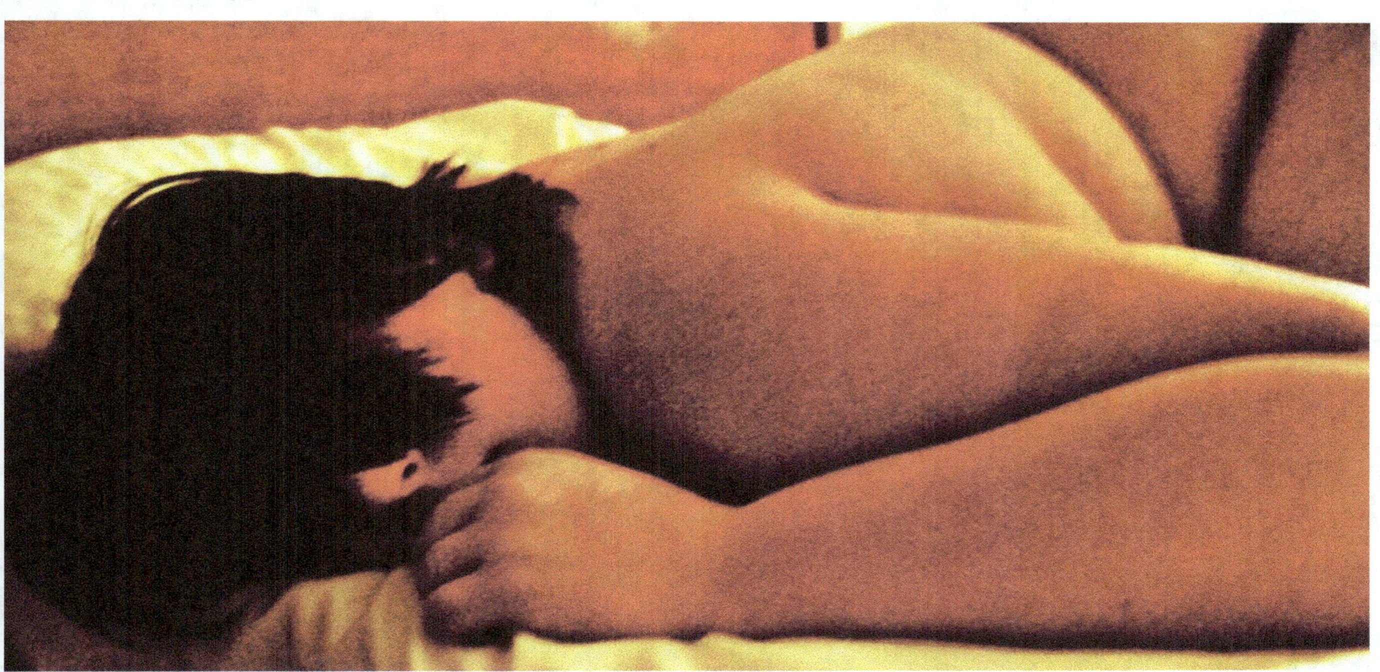

A person lying down on a bed

AI-generated content may be incorrect.

ENSNARED

By John Tustin

The Craftsman saw her one day –

her, the Jewelrymaker,

peeking as he did at her from his rearview mirror,

where he admired his own pretty and uninhibited profundity;

seeing himself, seeing himself and her –

her always in the backseat; a little smaller,

not quite in focus, softened features and

him always staring back at her,

the steering wheel on Cruise Control.

She loved the Craftsman –

she, the Jewelry Maker,

she saw something in him,

something that just had to be there

because she willed it to be so.

Something that was the remnant of another:

something dangerous, sinister, intense,

innately attractive to such a girl

who was at once rebellious and profoundly afraid.

She pledged her love to him and he swore back to her

with his fingers crossed behind his back,

nonchalant and controlled,

always the master of the situation.

Immediately and consistently,

he philandered and she forgave him.

This happened again and again,

over years and at various addresses,

as if rehearsed and restaged.

Upon his hundredth infidelity,

she left The Craftsman

and set herself adrift in the world

that seemed to belong to him

and men much like him.

Still, she ensnared The Craftsman's heart

with her eyes

and ensnared his fingers

with her wavy tresses (she called them tresses)

strewn along the pillow of their marital bed.His mind ensnared by her voice

and her body
and her,
her all of her,
in spite of the granite of his heart
and the hard dullness of his wants.
He pushed her away,
yet he could not let go of her.
He began to truly want her
just at the moment she fled him.
He grew sick and red with obsession,
relentlessly pursuing her during her facsimile of freedom.
She always loved The Poet; meanwhile,
all the while,
even when she was with The Craftsman:
ever since her teeny bopper days (which is what she called
those years that she was not a girl anymore
and not yet a woman,
or perhaps she was both at once.)
She knew him, The Poet, when he was smitten with another,
her own sister,
and he thought of her, The Jewelrymaker, as he would have
his own sister (if he had one) during those days,
her teeny bopper days.
She yearned to be The Muse as well as The Jewelrymaker –
on his pedestal alone,
alone above him,
painted from every conceivable angle,
looking down as his words for her ascended,
flowed around her,
lay supplicant at her feet
but there was no one to read to her
mad and earnest sonnets to her beauty
as the moonlight shone alabaster on her tawny skin
and the sea breeze sprinkled salt water
all along her wavy and flowing hair.
She deserved these sonnets. She deserved them
and she craved them,
thinking about them as she stared out of various windows,
before, during and after her the time with her philandering,

suave Craftsman.

The beauty of her lying stagnant in the linoleum light,

dropped there in the vastness of nothing

and exquisitely, delicately, relentlessly sad.

All she wanted was a poet who would write pretty words about her

and mean them and live them

and they would live together, just two,

the man who put down the words

and the woman for whom those words existed.

Then,

as The Jewelrymaker (to become The Muse) was adrift,

she saw him also adrift,

flowing again into her orbit –

The Poet:

the sad Poet, sick with his own delirious sadness,

clutching onto nothing more than survival

and the vaguest sanctity for life.

She remembered his kindness,

his wounded eyes of childhood,

his innocent but lusty demeanor.She then ensnared The Poet's heart

with her eyes

and ensnared his fingers

with her waving tresses, (she called them tresses)

flowing in the winking of the moonlight.

His mind ensnared by her voice

and her body

and her –

her all of her.

He floated: dumbly staring and reaching for her,

The Muse trapped in her tower,

yet somehow also adrift in the sea:

The Poet long broken down, torn up

but then gathered together again

and rebuilt with the help of The Muse.

He smashed down the door

in the tower where she was trapped, waiting,

waiting for something, waiting for him,

waiting for nothing but the passage of time

and then they swam to shore together,

huffing and coughing,

out of shape from all those years inert

and there they were together,

ocean-slicked,

thick-chested and heaving in harmony on the shore.

Then, one day,

a day no more or less innocuous as any other,

they were lying on the shore together,

sandy and soaked,

staring up at the stars that were as countless

as the many facets of her reflected heart

and her eyes both dark and secretive

and then, in an instant, she was gone –

leaving only a note on the bathroom mirror,

stating that things were good

until they weren't good anymore.

He didn't understand.

It was all still so good to him,

as he felt he was still living it.

Then,

toward the end of her time with The Poet –

her turn now to be the sinner, the philanderer:

she ensnared The Sailor's heart

with her eyes

and ensnared his fingers

with her wavy tresses (she called them tresses)

that floated in the water all around his vessel.

His mind ensnared by her voice

and her body

and her-

her all of her.

She, now the confused Mermaid (and still the Jewelrymaker/Muse)

with the poor, dim and soon-to-be dismissed Sailor.

She met him and she drank his wine,

coming to shore together for a moment

after flirting from afar for a seeming eternity –

him at the mast for months,

scanning the dark water,

the always-distant promise of land;

her emerging before him,

above the waterline, topless,

waving her tailfin to all of the sailors

from the false anonymity

of distant tropical rocks.

Her wanting nothing but to net their dual desire

and getting that, finally.

He was chosen from among all the sailors

to be the one to come to shore with her

and he kissed her once, twice;

touched her there and there

and then she was gone:

leaving only the scent of their comingled perspiration and lust;

a trace of the wine she drank imprinted on his lips;

a small ripple from her submerging tailfin

remaining seemingly forever in the water,

growing weaker and more distant.

The sailor sailed away from the mirage,

back to the anonymity of the ocean.

He saw her, he held her briefly;

the Mermaid he thought he had captured;

and then she was gone.

She then returned to The Craftsman;

no longer The Jewelrymaker or The Muse or the Mermaid

but merely The Dutiful One.

She no longer made beautiful things

to fall loosely from necks and wrists

and she no longer saw words made just for her,

sparking about her in the dark

and her tailfin had fallen to the bottom of the ocean,

rotting and rusting

along with the other detritus of the sea.

They made love but there was no love:

it was all a falsehood.

She closed her eyes and pretended The Poet was on top of her,

pulsing between her legs,

whispering his filth, hot in her ear,

looking through her the way he did:

seeing her but not seeing her,

the way he always would,

the way he always will.

She could not stop thinking of his words

or his eyes

or how she left him, more hopeless than she had found him.

The Craftsman, the unfaithful Craftsman,

he tried, he did.

His heart ensnared

by her eyes

and his fingers ensnared

by her waving tresses (she called them tresses.)

His mind ensnared by her voice

and her body

and her –

her all of her;

just as shackled as the others before and after him.

One day he woke up, reached for her

and she was gone.

Gone again.

She was gone and he understood

but he still wanted her;

only because he could not bear another

having her.

Another touching her would kill him

although his own touch chilled her now

and he knew this,

but still...

So,

she then went back to The Poet:

She, the reluctant Jailer (Jewlerymaker/Muse/Mermaid/Dutiful One)

And him now The Prisoner.

trapped in his thoughts of her, belief in her;

knowing she was likely the death of everything warm inside of him.

His hands dirty and strong from so much work,

her mind smoothing over and sheened from the unrepentant sameness of days;

his forearms twines of knots, his legs nothing but cramping ache.

When they met again, they tried to be friends this time,

their third time knowing each other,

instead of resparking lovers.

Upon their new goodbye the first night,

they threw away the script

and kissed and kissed atop the steps

that led downward to his oblivion of without her.

They had to. Sometimes the script is nothing more than a suggestion

when passion takes hold,

takes control in spite of common sense

and all those fingers pointing.

The Prisoner and The Jailer,

locked together in the same asylum.

Lips and eyes locked together in that moment thought eternal;

bodies locked together in the night

under that same oblivious moon.His heart ensnared

by her eyes

and his fingers ensnared

in her waving tresses (she called them tresses.)

His mind ensnared by her voice

and her body

and her –

her always and inevitable her.

Just like then, those few years ago,

the meeting again that led to their lifelong connection.

They took the train from the city to his bed

and he saw her beneath him and above him,

in the simmering heat inside the darkness,

the golden slatted moonlight shafting on the bed;

holding her hair in one hand,

her hip in another,

all of it flowing through his fingers

like sand or water

and kissing her and kissing her,

staring into the core of her,

wan but enflamed

as he put it in and she took it,

pliant and soft and yet so recalcitrant.

He noticed the new harshness of her,

the paint chipped, edges scuffed,

the new scars she bore,

self-inflicted all.

He held her again

and even in his happiness,

he knew that she would remain The Jailer

and he The Prisoner

until she could free herself from her own bondage.

She could not release him until she herself was free.

Her hair shook in the jarring sadness

of the pitched blackness of the night

and he stared into the blackness of her eyes,

her waves of her, her heart,

her everything.

His legs weak, eyes trembling,

eyes limp,

everything he felt and knew was true was a lie

but still, it was beyond his control

and even his mind's fathoming;

he simply had to have her,

although she was a slave to her self-proclaimed duty

and he would always be a prisoner of her –

her black black tresses (she called them tresses)

that showed through red in the sunlight

and those mysterious and secretive

almost-black eyes.

She would always be his muse –

The Muse;

but in trying to be everything to everyone,

she was not quite anything to anyone

except a part of their unhappiness,

their unfulfillment

swirling and mixing with her own.She has played every role,

all of her selves acting out each part

and, every time,

she has failed.

A drawing of a person holding a swing

Daisy Renee Photography

Delicate Burning of My Heart

By Bobbi Sinha-Morey

As if an angelic light had been
stolen from my life I palely
realized what I hoped for the
most will never come again,
the most delicate burning of
my heart wasting away any
wishes I've ever made. Open
air is for the living, not my
enervated hushed soul while
I impatiently sew my prayers
together, left with the smell
of dusty velvet and time I put
away for the drudgery it takes
to carry on living and whether it
lasts or silences me I'll dolefully
wait. I used to tie knots in the
half-lives of blossoms, paint
tomorrow's sky in my dreams.
My days are strung together
listening to the wind lay bare
the willow trees.

Onetime Miracle

By Bobbi Sinha-Morey

No miraculous luck will ever
fall in my lap again; it had been
a onetime miracle as if there
were a limit set in heaven.
I had cried the day it came and
now it felt like the sting of a wasp
knowing that my only dream like
a red diamond had been crushed
to bits. No ounce of hope will
sustain me, my heart left raw
and bare. I search corners for
any scrap of light as days pass,
enveloped in infinite silences
where words used to be, and
I raise my eyes to an absent god,
knowing my prayers were thrown
against the wall, the dust of my
life sobering me to stamp out
any belief that my dream will
ever happen. Remembrance
of what I once had is now
a left-over gift of the mind
leaving me impatient, wishing
I could do without. When I lay
in bed at night a lifetime of
despondency swallows me.

Dove-Grey Dawns

By Bobbi Sinha-Morey

In the tenebrous days before me
it was a dream that so barely
survived til its tiny flame silently
died and I hardly knew the feeling
of being alive anymore. Dove-grey
dawns replaced the sun; an unseen
finger opened the door to let out
the tears, the future no longer
awaiting me anymore; only an
invisible pin fastening me to
the present leaving me enough
room left to breathe, but no space
to be wild as the wind as I used to
be. I grew used to the movements
of existence, a burden that felt like
the longest stage in life before death.
There were no panoply of highlights;
they were hidden away from me like
untouchable, glimmering red jewels.
If I even escape this meager life with
nowhere to go except to grow old
I'd reach for the only hand that had
given me love and remember its
light, carry it with me til I peacefully,
forever, close my eyes.

Still Fingers

By Tom Barlow

The son returns the finger sizer to me
with four of her jeweled gold rings:
two diamonds, a garnet and a ruby, all
too small for her fingers now. Old
skin dust dulls the pavilion of each gem,
but nothing the steam won't clean.
One by one I hold them in the bench pin,
use the jeweler's saw to cut the ring shank.
Pliers pull the sides apart like mourners'
hands at the end of a service, then
the needle file straightens up the sides
of the cut. Calipers measure bench stock
to add to the back of the ring and then
comes solder and the torch—so fitting
that flames help bridge the gap—
and into the pickle pot. Then the file
again and the flex shaft with the coarse
sandpaper bit and then emery paper.
The rawhide mallet and mandrel
beat the rings round again.
The dull finish of the tripoli polish
would be enough for her, most would
say, given the short time she'll wear
these rings, but I take rouge to the
buffing wheel and make them shine,
for I know this woman by her rings
and by such totems we all survive.

the middle finger of my left hand *after Aracelis Girmay*

By Terry Jude Miller

curves to the right—balances

an arthritic road with a touch

of poetic justice—it is king

of guitar chords—rests

on the keyboard's letter D—but

not for long—off to eat E and C

and occasionally 3—it is the index

finger's companion—they are in love

but hide their romance—cousin

of the thumb and rival of the pinky

more often in my fiery younger days

it was the implement of my anger

when I'd taken offense—rightly

or not—to some road-raged driver

on Houston's Southwest Freeway

my two-year-old grandson calls

him March—the month not the motion

I—on the other hand—have not named

him—it seems inappropriate to give labelto something so magnificent—so necessary

to share this poem

the distance between a ghost and an angel is a lifetime

By Terry Jude Miller

sargassum of pink clouds

stretches across the summer skybreeze through my beard

fingers to the flesh beneath

the wind says it is alright

I turned out this way—

worried I never

cared enough—didn't fill

this lifetime with the proper

amount of pity for others we do the best we can to be better than the person we fell asleep as

it turns out—that's the only competition

worth perspiration

today the world gives me weather I can use

light—breeze—shared

with the trees that shade

me—I wonder if they

wonder too

the imposter

By Terry Jude Miller

"I barely survived the trauma of my childhood, and was mostly dissociative, stoned, and numb while getting my undergrad. My college experience was so riddled with rejection and shame, being kicked out of the Corps of Cadets at Texas A&M for being gay, being hazed, drug abuse as self medication, and suicidal ideations and attempts. I was trying so hard just not to end myself." – Kai Coggin

writers don't get tiredthey get even

masters of the impossible imposter

they shift and sift through sadness

to find art—to make art—to have art

make them

they arrive at the self

that is always arriving

are in constant wardrobe-change

in unending makeup-call

ear cocked for their cue

when they are gonetheir words are volumes left behindfor the next imposter

to find and balance

the world on a pen-prick

of art

After the Breakup, We Are Roommates
By James Croal Jackson
What have we learned? Anything? Oh god,
the disaster of living, being roommates
now after years of *forever.* The PhDs
we have in each other lost value. The mental
state has alternate rights. What was the system
you asked to inspect? Oh yes, tradition.
We would prove everyone wrong,
including ourselves. Forget
to vacuum our dead cat's fur from
the stairs. Leave greasy pans in
the sink to soak– in the soak
to sink. Every day
a rattling ghost jumps
out from holes in the walls
we still must spackle.

Layna Williams

Kingdom

By James Croal Jackson

I bet you have

a mansion. You sell

land at true

cost– blood-

soaked

beasts,

all the kingdom

in your pocket,

the precious

metals

polished

at your feet,

hungry stars needing

forever

more. I wish

that for you– my hunger

tastes of bitter

rosemary,

the dreams

of a plot

go on through

the storm.

The National Center for Anti-Corporate Activism

By James Croal Jackson

I cannot live in modern society

I want more fruits of labor

I want to look more deeply

at holes in the earth

I will start a revolution

in a grass hut in the middle of the Rockies

called the National Center for Anti-Corporate Activism

we will spend less time finding meaning

and more time making homemade ice cream

and in our quest for deliciousness

we will want the best ingredients

fresh cream eggs chocolate peanut butter sugar

we will live simpler lives

no more gadgets and elaborate hotels

only going to the library

or the rainforest

or the Grand Canyon

to look at squirrels

who live like us

sustainable lifestyles

dirt-free

boredom and beauty

we will defeat corporations

we will control our lives

they will– I'm

sorry–

buy our ideas

bury them

Potions

By Layna Williams

I come from drops of sweat,

broken crayons peeled and shaved,

small flowers collected at recess,

a spray of my mothers perfume

that I had to sneak once her boyfriend had left the room,

and cold water from the bathtub

The water heater was broken

I sit in my bedroom floor,

hunched over a small cup meant for oral medication

In it I smush my ingredients together using an unsharpened pencil

Pushing the color out of my flowers, being careful not to let the smell of perfume

be overwhelmed by the sweat,

Forgotten on my belly

by the man who interrupted Scooby Doo

to spend time with me again

This is important!

I stir until nothing keeps on happening

Realizing

it's just a tiny cup

filled with sweat,

crayons,

flowers,

perfume

and cold water

I flushed it down the toilet.

Release

Elizabeth?

Skeleton hanging from a door frame

Petrified tendons play a waiting game

Till it's nothing but a skull

And a tight rope strung up from the a frame

Bones ground to dust like rust

Cover up the floor

But it can't smother all this self blame

All the waiting, praying, drowning in doubt and shame

There's not a steeple I could find

To put my head under for a while

No pews for repentance

Just repugnant fake smiles

The whole world seems plastic

And melting, on fire

I breathe in the toxins

Now it's my turn to smile

Bricks and boards

Callous my shoulders

It's like the whole world

Could topple over

If i miss a step

It's all over

I try to rest

But the world just smolders

Angels losing feathers

While I process the damage

Collect, assess, readjust, manage

And I'm bending from my bones

Bursting at the seams

I don't care to fit in

But i wonder what all this shit means

Sometimes I want to fall in a lake

Buy a guillotine

Crawl in a fucking hole and die

But my vengeance rips and screams

I'm here out of spite

Take a bat to your knees

The only thing I want

Is to truly be free

Aquarius

By Kelly Ann Wilson

Women of the water

Sea salt is our perfume

You can find us by the seashore

Painting with every shade of blue

We sing an untamed siren's song

But take a mermaid's form

Look deeper than the surface

At the late January born

Wolves

By Kelly Ann Wilson

Oh, so small and delicate too

Is a young girl born into our world

So, from the moment she opens her green eyes

She's at the mercy of the wolves

It's true, for a time, they are bigger and stronger

And they know it

And throughout her life, she comes to learn

They will take every chance they have to show it

All so instinctively, she reaches for the ones

The ones who ought to keep her safe

Until the first time that they let her down

All to save a man's name

And so then, she wanders on her own

Searching for the next thing and the next

She clings to what might protect her just for a minute

So she can let down her guard and rest

You see, it hasn't changed, it's a scary place

Even as she's grown older

Now, she's a woman on a dimly lit street

And that's where the hunters hunt her

After all, the way things are was written by men

Not a little girl with something to say

Hex the patriarchy that seeks to slowly

Take pieces of her along the way

A little bit of her voice, a little bit of her power

A little bit of her courage, of her brilliant mind

But she won't let them take what's hers

And all the ways she is meant to shine

She'll keep soft edges

Where scar tissue wants to form

She'll still light up at wondrous things she loves

In defiance of their scorn

And while the Earth around her burns with division and hate

She'll show her good and kind heart without fear

Though she knows there are wolves out there

She remains a delicate deer

Fury

By Kelly Ann Wilson

I wrote songs

I read books

I educated

I ran

I offered solace to survivors

I listened to lectures

I signed petitions

I buried my feet in the cool sand

I breathed through meditations

I ate dark chocolate

I renovated an old house

I studied

I listened to the waves crash

I got on my yoga mat

I sang "Mad Woman" at the top of my lungs

I went to therapy

I wore tourmaline crystals on my wrist

I painted

I hiked through the forest

I saved someone else from all of the things

I can never go back and save myself from.

I did every single thing I could do

With my fury.

Except what you did

With yours.

The Strength in Submission

Push me

To my limits

Push me past

Teach me what

my body can do

How much

I can take

No one

Has ever seen me

As strong

Until you

Saw someone

Who could kneel

Who could handle

The sting

The thump

The slap

The pull

Someone whose body

Was stronger than

She ever imagined

Someone whose mind

Could overcome

The pain to

Find the pleasure

Past what I

Thought were my

Limits

To a place where

In your hands

I can do

Anything

A person sitting in front of a pot of magic

A person holding a lit candle

AI-generated content may be incorrect.

A person in a mask holding a knife

AI-generated content may be incorrect.

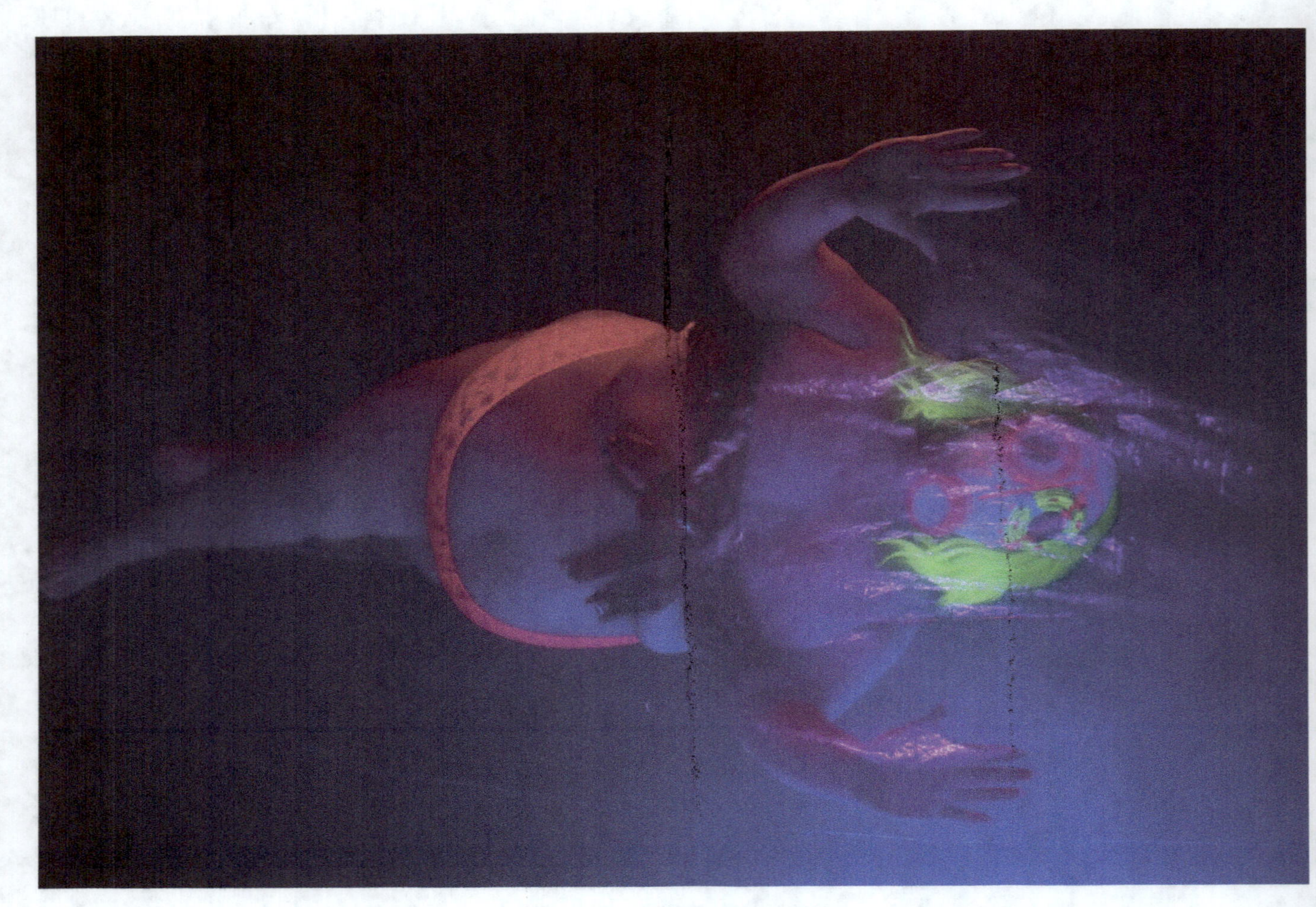

HOUSE OF OPEN ROOMS

By Toni Scales

On Thursdays the words fall from my lips like adjectives for water. Dark, dirty. Breaking. The garage door won't unhinge, its swollen chains where the grease and slide abandoned us long ago. How we try to mend all the wingless butterflies, end up singeing their hearts with the matches in our ears. Besides, they're too small for our fingers, go sticking against pink fluorescent tape and cherry diamond rings. Somehow it's familiar, it's like the way I love, limbs that pop and bleed against all that adhering.

I'll become a victim every two seconds. Upstairs there's a calamity, a cacophony, yellow roses like hands trembling in vases. I am fascinated, fanatical. Fastened to pain like a button. How the tightness makes me shudder. My depression has a little white church and white sheets in the backyard. A bell that rings when you're hungry. That rings when the weather's slightly off.

We are docile and ladylike, prone to high stimulation. In the kitchen my mother chops too hard at lettuce. Says there are things I'll never know and keeps opening and closing her arms. Something about peonies and peroxide. Or scentless soap and scissors. Somewhere a woman hangs a picture and bites her bottom lip. Slides like a letter into the clean envelope of the coverlet and places her palms on her belly. The wallpaper resembling a pattern like the ocean or my unstable relationships, storms and grey drizzle pelting tiny swaying ships. My self image glazed and distorted as beach glass. In my bed a rash of paroxysms and purple satin pillows. Of longing and Ciara cloying in the sheets.

In my head too many people are wearing flowered sun hats and traveling with candles and whispering psalms and litanies from aged green cupboards. Still no one wants to invite them in. I was raised to tell no one, though I admit I caused the little ivory bible I kept hidden under the mattress to go swerving down the river. There's a constant fever, a sense of pulling in. I'm tortured by sleep-deprivation and porcelain angels, silver light scattering from heart-shaped bulbs. Your sweet little hell I let back into me. I can sniff your cruelty from miles away, practically feel the intaglio of veins in your arms. You always knew there was something left of me on the roof that flickered in the rain. A voice crooning from deep in the forest, Don't fret. There will come a day when the cows stop trampling and the crying will end. When everything inside and out of you will forget.

Out With A Bang

By Joe Shaw

Gunpowder tasted sweet to Martin. He didn't know why, but he liked it. He pulled it out of his mouth and placed the gun back into his inside jacket pocket before returning to the party.

Martin was a man of few words. He had spent his entire life working in a small town, building his business, and raising his family. Now, at the age of 70, he was finally retiring, and it was time for his farewell party. He hated it. The idea that he would no longer be needed burned at the back of his consciousness. So he made a plan to go out in style.

As the day drew nearer, Martin became more and more nervous. He wasn't used to being the center of attention, and he wasn't sure what to expect. But when the day finally arrived, he was pleasantly surprised.

The party was held in a local park, and all of Martin's friends and family were there. They had brought food and drinks, and everyone was in good spirits. Martin walked around, shaking hands and chatting with his guests. He felt a warmth in his heart that he had never experienced before.

Soon, it was time for the speeches. Martin's son stood up and talked about all the things his father had accomplished over the years and how proud he was to have him as a dad. Martin's wife spoke next. She talked about how much she loved him and how grateful she was for all the sacrifices he had made to provide for their family. Martin was taken aback. He had operated for so many years under the illusion that nobody truly cared for him, that life was just a sham, and that everyone was simply after his money. But his guests and family showed true emotion; their care and love for Martin were genuine. Despite this, he felt he had to press on with his plan. It was too late at this point.

At the end of the speeches, Martin stood up to have his own speech, something his family and guests hadn't expected. He was nervous at first but soon found his stride. He talked about all the people he had met over the years and how much he had enjoyed building his business in their town. He thanked everyone for coming and promised that he would never forget this day. Raising a glass to end his speech, he spoke his last words.

"Truly, the only regret I have now is the massive amount of poison I added to everyone's food and drinks here tonight. But alas, I will be with you all shortly," Martin said, reaching into his jacket to retrieve his pistol.

It was true that Martin was a man of few words. But he sure knew how to throw a party, and he went out with a bang. The last thing that went through his head, other than the bullet, was how sweet the gunpowder tasted.

The Enchanted Forest Beckons

By Robert Tustin

The sun was just beginning its ascent, casting a golden hue over the village of Rook Hollow. The cobblestone streets were quiet, save for the gentle hum of morning life stirring awake. Robins chirped their dawn chorus, and the scent of dew-kissed flowers filled the air. It was in this tranquil setting that Orbert, the half-elf bard, found his inspiration.

Orbert strolled through the village square, his ukulele slung over his shoulder. The bronze mermaid fountain in the center of the square glistened with morning light, its waters trickling down melodically into the half shell bowl that formed its base. Orbert paused, taking in the serenity of the scene. This was his routine, a morning walk to clear his mind and invite the muses to visit him.

His path took him to the edge of the village, where the cobblestones gave way to a well-trodden dirt path leading into the enchanted forest. The forest was a place of magic and mystery, where the ordinary and the extraordinary coexisted. It was here that Orbert often found the spark for his poetry and songs.

As he stepped into the forest, a sense of calm washed over him. The trees, tall and ancient, seemed to whisper secrets of old. Sunlight filtered through the canopy, casting dappled shadows on the forest floor. Orbert's fingers instinctively strummed a soft melody on his ukulele, harmonizing with the natural symphony around him.

Orbert wandered deeper, his heart attuned to the forest's magic. He paused by a familiar grove, where a cluster of glowing flowers grew. These flowers, known as Lumina Blooms, were one of the forest's many wonders. Their petals glowed softly, even in daylight, and their nectar was the source of the enchanted honey produced by Thistle Bumbleshade's bees, known colloquially as Elderglow Bees, but most everywhere else as Rook Hollow honeys.

He knelt beside the blooms, gently touching a petal. The glow intensified, and Orbert smiled, feeling a surge of inspiration. He began to hum a new tune, one that captured the essence of the Lumina Blooms and the magic they held.

Lost in his music, Orbert didn't notice the figure watching him from the shadows. Sharra, the witch who lived in the guest house of the haunted mansion on the outskirts of the village, had been drawn to the grove by the enchanting melody. She stayed hidden, her dark eyes fixed on Orbert. There was a part of her that loathed his carefree spirit and the joy he found in the forest. Yet, another part of her, a part she rarely acknowledged, was captivated by his music.

Orbert stood and continued his walk, unaware of Sharra's presence. He made his way to a clearing where a grand linden tree stood. This was Hal, the awakened tree who had witnessed centuries of the forest's history and who had been struck by lightning more times than he cared to mention. Hal's branches rustled as Orbert approached, a silent greeting between old friends.

"Good morning, Hal," Orbert said, sitting at the base of the tree. "I know you're sensitive about them but your scars really do add to your boundless charm." He played a cheerful tune, one that Hal seemed to enjoy. The leaves rustled in time with the music, creating a gentle, harmonious duet.

"Thank you, old friend," replied Hal, " I appreciate the kind words."

As the music filled the clearing, Orbert felt a sense of fulfillment. Here, amidst the magic of the forest, he was at peace. The melodies came easily, each note a reflection of the beauty around him. He closed his eyes, letting the music flow, unaware that the enchanted forest held more secrets and surprises than he could ever imagine.

Unbeknownst to Orbert, his morning serenades had attracted more than just the attention of the witch. The forest itself seemed to respond to his music, the magic within its depths stirring and awakening. The enchanted bees buzzed around the Lumina Blooms, their hum adding a new layer to the symphony. And somewhere, deep within the forest, a soft, almost imperceptible glow began to pulse in rhythm with Orbert's tune.

The enchanted forest beckoned, its magic whispering promises of inspiration and adventure. Orbert's heart swelled with the possibilities that lay ahead. Little did he know, this was just the beginning of a journey that would lead him to discover the true heart of Rook Hollow and the hidden depths of his own soul.

Kendra Matott

Last Supper

By Dan Keeble

Camp Commandant Eduard Koch fingered the silver picture frame on his desk. A blonde girl of about nine years old was in a rowing boat, laughing at her daddy struggling with the oars. Miriam's own daughter had been about the same age when taken from her at Flossenbürg.

She put the plate in front of the commandant, who tucked a napkin into the neck of his SS tunic. He waved her away with a flick of his hand. She had made sure that he never saw that smiling child's face again.

His hut was the same size as hers. Except it didn't house twenty-eight impoverished souls sleeping three high on rough hewn bunks without mattresses. Neither did it make you retch from the stench of perishing bodies, malnourished and ravaged by dysentery, fleas, and the lack of basic sanitation afforded to farm animals.

No, his hut had warmth from a stove. Flags and nurturing tapestries from the Motherland adorned the walls, with an opulent red plush sofa and velvet seated chairs.

Miriam had stewed the beef and carrots. To soften the cabbage the way the commandant demanded, she added baking soda. German soldiers had been using caustic soda of late to clear the drains. Over the space of weeks, she had collected enough from the spillages around the gratings to make up a small package to sneak into the kitchen to add to the baking soda.

Ambling back to her hut, Miriam looked up at a reddening sky, knowing it would soon reunite her with her daughter.

I Saw a Man

By Clyde Liffey

Whenever I go somewhere that is new to me, I try to visit the cemeteries. I gaze not so much at the descriptions on the headstones – a failure in business, he mistreated – as at the names of the deceased and their birth and death dates. This, I convince myself, gives me a true sense of the ethos of the place. Far enough away from the Snows, Greens, and Dales where I live, I leant against the railing surrounding an old churchyard when I saw him.

He's not the type of person I normally associate with. Of middling height, extraordinarily thin, unwashed, with unruly hair and a staring unworldly countenance – most avoid him. I'm not sure why, maybe the serenity that ensues a walk among the dead, but something within me drew him towards me. I didn't ignore him. He walked quickly but would often suddenly stop to explain, exclaim, vent. I believe he was offering me a tour of the village, something I'd feel obliged to tip him for. I was about to decline – after all reception for my phone was adequate here – when I noticed an acquaintance across the way.

The Black man with a trim moustache and maybe a goatee did a double take when he saw us. He remembered me as much as I remembered him, I guess. We were both in town for a regional user conference that began early next morning. The wild man noticed how we regarded each other, paused. My colleague hesitated, reluctant to approach. I noted the contrast in the facial hair of our trio: my new companion had a beard almost long enough for birds to nest in, the co-visitant groomed his beard and moustache, I was clean-shaven for I shave even on weekends and vacations. Absent-minded, I ran my fingers over cheeks and chin, wondered if I remembered to pack my razor. I retraced my morning steps, couldn't remember placing the blades in my pouch, how late on Sundays were the stores open here? did the hotel have spares? what impression was I making on the man across the street? Of course we'd interact tomorrow, we may even breakfast together!

He disappeared in search of a meal or some other entertainment. You know of course of the shameful way people in this town treated Blacks, the young man resumed. People in the South, I'm not apologizing for slavery, but at least they acknowledged Africans, lived, worked, begat with them, whereas here they took the land from the indigenous people, allowed no Blacks, not even domestics. It's not just New England towns like this of course, the Constitution, I'm digressing, it's time for reparations. I had my genes traced. I've got traces of African blood, Native American blood, even Neanderthal! We always denigrate the Neanderthals and yet our forebears – come, I'll show you the Civil War monument.

I could already see it a few blocks away; we weren't in a big town, not in Salem, somehow, he got on to witch dunkings and drownings, he grabbed my arm, I recoiled. He strode down the street, I like to amble, we hadn't gone half a block when I stopped. I saw a patch of swaying Queen Anne's lace, small-petaled daisies, weeds, some Russian sage-like plant in the space between two house boundaries. That's the extent of wildness you get here, he said, a strand here, a strand there, we'll choke not on climate change but on domesticity. There's no Nature here. Neither of those adjoining homeowners owns that strip of land and so neither mows it. Once their petty dispute is settled, the flowers will go. If you want to see Nature in its rawest form, look at the super-rich.

We went on, he raving and gesticulating, me looking at the storefront windows, was that a pharmacy we passed? until we arrived at the statue. We were the only people there. Look familiar? he asked.

It looks like any other Civil War statue I've seen.

Have you seen any in the South?

Yes.

Exactly! he said. Those monuments were all made by the same company. They just changed the initials on the belt buckle. Those initials were faded now. It's all about money in this country. The Civil War wasn't fought to free the slaves, it was a battle of the North's monied people against the South's, Blacks and Irish be damned! There were now some people about, no Blacks that I could see, some Irish or part

Irish most likely. No one seemed surprised by his rant. I guess they were used to it. I examined his beard while he garbled his manufactured facts. There was salad dressing in it, the white ranch so popular these days. He's a wild man who capitalizes on the Dumpsters outside the village restaurants, I thought.

He ceased, out of breath, aware of my cynicism. A drop of sweat glistened on my otherwise calm brow. Red-faced, fists clenched then raised, he gasped, collected himself. I felt in my pocket for singles for I was sure that a few bucks tip would end our commerce. I withdrew my hand from my pocket, looked up, and saw that he'd run on.

A drawing of an eye

Road Kill

By Eve Lyons

At first I don't even see it. It's Sunday afternoon, after religious school, and before the usual family brunch. My mom comes in and plops the paper down in front of me. I'm looking at the Montgomery Ward coupons folded around the front page and the Sears Roebuck ad that has fallen onto the floor, and I look at her like, what?

"He's in your class, right?" she says. Then in the same breath, "I got muffins and bagels for brunch. Which one do you want?"

"Muffin," I say, scanning the front page hurriedly. Up in the top right hand corner is a picture of a twelve-year-old boy. That's Jason Kim three years ago, I think. What's Jason doing on the front page? I scan the headlines. 'Reagan Gives Qaddafi Ultimatum.' '2 Heights Teens Killed on I-37.' There's a whole story, which I don't really read, and a map showing exactly where on I-37 they were killed, and a side bar - I know that's what it's called cause I'm in Mrs. Johnson's Journalism class - about how teens shouldn't ever drink cause we're so irresponsible. Whatever. I wad up the paper into a tiny ball and hurl it into the trash can across the room. My mom is going to be pissed I threw away the front page, but I don't care. It made me mad.

I lie back down on my bed and try not to think about what I've just read. I'm thinking about religious school this morning, and how Jeremy Davis told me Jason wants to ask me to the Homecoming dance next week. It can't be true, is all I can think. Maybe someone at the paper is playing a joke. I'm sure Jason'll be there when I go to school tomorrow. He'll probably sidle up to my locker like he's been doing all this week and finally shyly ask me to the Homecoming dance. I want to call his house and prove this is all a sick prank, but I'm scared. Scared it's not.

I reach over to my bedside table and pick up my phone and press MEM 1. Andrea will know what's going on.

"Hey, Andrea. It's Kate, " I say.

"Kate, hi," she says, "Look, can I call you right back? Jenny's on the other line. I think she's having a crisis."

Jenny's always having a crisis. This is really important though. This is big. "This is really important, Andrea, " I say, "Did you read the paper this morning?"

"No, why?" she asks. She sounds impatient.

"Well, it says that like - " I begin. I realize I have no idea what to say, "There's this article that talks about - well, it says that Jason died."

"Jason who?" Andrea asks. Like she doesn't even care. Like it's no big deal.

"Jason Kim."

"He's the one who's always at your locker, right?" she asks.

"Yeah. He's in my second period history class. Some other boy died too. Some guy from Clark."

"What happened?"

"They got into a car accident. I guess the guy from Clark was drunk."

"Well shit, no wonder," Andrea sounds relieved. Like the fact that he was drinking makes it OK that they died. I guess she can't believe it either. When we were thirteen we found out our fifth grade teacher died of lung cancer. Andrea just said "Well, he was old" and wouldn't say any more. I know she missed him though, because she stopped eating for a week. But she just kept saying "I'm fine, just fine" so many times we all knew she wasn't. Her parents eventually paid like thousands of dollars for her to go to Cedar Ridge until she agreed to eat. Andrea's parents can afford it, though. They're loaded. Eventually Andrea started eating, but she never admitted what was wrong.

I guess she's going to do the same thing about Jason Kim.

"I guess," is all I say. I don't know what to say to her. I want to tell her to make sure she eats, but I'm afraid she'll get mad at me. We haven't talked about that since it happened.

"Listen, Kate, I've got to go," Andrea says, "I've got Jenny on the other line. She's freaking out."

"All right," I start to hang up, "See you tomorrow."

Practically as soon as I lay down, my finger still holding the hang-up button, my mom screeches for me to come to brunch. I can hear my brother's squeaky cheap Payless shoes beating me to the table. Little brown noser.

But I don't feel like going to brunch. Suddenly I don't feel like I can eat. I have this heavy nauseated feeling in my stomach. I run to the bathroom down the hall and don't quite make it. Last night's mac and cheese mostly makes it into the toilet and a little on the floor. When I'm done I've got a chunk of barf on my cheek and the whole bathroom smells awful. I wash myself up and head into the dining room, still feeling queasy.

"Hey stinky," the Toad says as soon as he sees me. My mom gives me this look like, how many times have I told you to come when you're called?

The whole dining room reeks of eggs, which doesn't help my queasy feeling. I know I have to get out of there, and fast. "Mom, I've got to go out," I say. She looks at me like I just sprouted a third arm, "I feel really sick, and I need to think."

She comes over to me, and kind of tugs me into the kitchen like she's going to tell me something top secret that my brother can't hear.

"Is this about that boy from your school?" she whispers.

I nod at her, afraid if I speak I'll hurl again. I wonder why she's whispering, why death is a big secret to keep from my brother. When the Toad was four and I was six our uncle died. I remember my mother wailing so loud I thought the whole world must have known. My father just sat around looking glum for weeks. Kind of like he looks today, kind of like he looks every Sunday at brunch time. He doesn't like family events much. Sometimes I wonder if he likes his family much.

"All right, sweetie," she holds me close to her, "What time will you be back?"I shrug. "Sixish?"

She lets me go, leaving my brother and father to stare and probably wonder what the hell is going on. I flip the Toad off subtly on my way out the door. Once I'm out the door, I feel better. Fresh air. Freedom. I don't even know where I'm going, I figure I'll just walk to Stop 'n' Drive or maybe my friend Jolie's house.

Jolie is so cool she scares me. She's kind of a freak at school. I used to think she was really pretty. But this year she has electric blue hair that's shaved on one side and she started dressing kind of weird. She wears tons of make-up and nothing but black clothes. Once I spent the night at her house, and I saw her closet. Practically everything in it was black! Except there's one dress, all blue and sparkly; she said her mother makes her wear it to family reunions.

Anyway, I'm half way to her house, which is ten blocks from my house, when I find a dead cat in the middle of the road. It has dried purplish-brown blood on it, and its tiny skull is smashed. Usually, I would look away; I can't stand the sight of blood and we have two cats. But today I don't look away. I don't know why. I peer closer, crouching down. Then I hop back up and start scouring someone's yard for flowers. I make a small bouquet of wildflowers and make a circle around the cat. I don't know. It seems so sad, knowing that grown-ups will just drive by and look and say, 'Oh that's terrible' and then never think of it again. I wonder whose cat it is; it's got a collar on. The tags are underneath its mangled body, but I manage to pull them out and look. R. S. Lowenstein. 114 Second Street. 824-3465. I stuff the tags inside my pocket and say good-bye to the cat, thinking about the street cleaners who will come and sweep it up tomorrow.

A few more blocks and I'm at Jolie's house. Her parents aren't often home, but when they are they scare me. Once Jolie's father slapped her so hard she fell over backwards. So I usually just sneak up to her bedroom window instead of going to the front door. Today I only have to tap once on the window before Jolie's nose is poking through two slats of the blinds. She grins and pulls up her shade and opens her window.

"Kate, what are you doing here?" she asks, "I thought you'd be at brunch."

"I told my mom I had to go out," I say. I can feel myself hesitating, I want to tell her about Jason, but she might not respond the right way. I'm not sure how I want her to respond - just not like Andrea, I guess.

"Well, come in."

I climb over the window sill and into her room. It's painted all black and she's got one tall lamp with a purple light bulb casting a weird glow all over. A year ago I asked my parents if I could paint my room black. My mom just laughed and my father roared "Absolutely not!" I didn't even really want to do it. I just wanted to know if my parents would let me.

"My parents are gone," Jolie says, "They went to Canyon Lake for the weekend."

"Cool! You should have a party," I say without thinking. I don't know who would come if Jolie had a party. Everyone at school pretty much thinks she's a weirdo. Brad Huggins says she's a slut who only sleeps with college guys. I think that might just be because he asked her out when we were in eighth grade and she told him 'no.' But I'm like her only friend, and I don't think she's even been out on date.

"Yeah, right," Jolie laughs.

"Jolie," I say seriously. She changes her tone instantly, like she can tell I'm about to say something that's not gossip. I love that about her.

"Jason Kim died." It comes out a lot easier if you just blurt it out. Each extra word I used when I told Andrea made my tongue drier.

"Oh hon," Jolie pulls me toward her and hugs me. I'm so surprised I forget what to do, then I kind of relax into her hug and let a few tears well up in my eyes. "Was he a good friend of yours?"

"Yeah," I say, "He was in my second period History class. He was really funny. He was always getting sent to the principal's office for making us laugh." I don't tell her about flirting at my locker, or how he was going to ask me to the dance. I don't even tell her I've known him since third grade. I don't know why.

"I think you mentioned him," Jolie says, holding my shoulders like she thinks I'll fall down if she doesn't. "I'm so sorry."

"Yeah," I say. What else can I say? I don't even know how to feel, or what to feel. Right now, I don't feel anything because it doesn't feel like it really happened. I wonder how I'll feel when I see his empty seat in History class. I wonder how I'll feel after two weeks of seeing his empty chair.

"Well, what do you feel like doing?" Jolie asks, "I mean, is there something that would make you feel better, or take your mind off this?" It sounds like she's reading the wrong cue card or something. What could possible make me feel better or make me forget that someone I just saw last Friday was no longer alive? I remember his house. In elementary school he invited me to his tenth birthday party. I thought it meant he liked me, so I picked him for square dancing that week. Turns out he invited the whole class. I used to be a bit of a dork.

"Kate? You in there?" Jolie is asking.

"What?" I ask.

"I said, let's go and make some lunch, OK? I'm starved."

We go into her kitchen and start fixing ourselves tuna fish sandwiches. I know Jolie's kitchen as well as she does; we're always fixing ourselves dinner. I don't think Jolie ever eats with her family. That's so cool. I tried to convince my mom we should all eat whenever we want but she said then we wouldn't be a family.

"You want to know what I want to do?" I ask as we start chowing down on our sandwiches, "I want to go here." I pull the cat tags out of my pocket and set them on the table.

"What's this?" Jolie pokes at the tags like they're diseased.

"Tags from this cat I saw. A cat got hit on Zapata street," I say.

"So what exactly do you want to do?"

"Find these people, the owners. Tell them what happened."

"Why?" Jolie looks appalled at the idea.

"I-I-I don't know," I'm caught off-guard. I haven't really thought it out this far yet, "So they can give it a proper funeral, or something. It just seems too horrible. Why can't people drive without hitting cats?"

"I don't know," Jolie shrugs defensively, "My dad hit a cat once. It was walking in the middle of the road at eleven at night. He just couldn't see it. I think the cats who get hit are probably pretty dumb."

Jolie pulls out a container of mustard and squeezes some on her finger. She eats mustard plain. It makes me ill to watch her, so instead I'm staring at the pastel puppy dog wallpaper in her kitchen.

"114 Second street," Jolie reads the tag. She gets mustard on it, so then she tries to wipe it off with the edge of her t-shirt, which is black of course. Black with some band that only stoners listen to on it, but it's got holes in it and paint on it so you really don't notice the smear of yellow mustard, "That's pretty close to here."

"So will you come with me?" I ask.

"Sure, I guess." She goes to the sink and washes her hands. I'm still finishing off my sandwich. But pretty soon after I do, we're out the door. Whenever I'm with Jolie we do things very decisively. It's so different from hanging out with Andrea and Jenny for two hours at the mall before we can decide we want to see a movie.

"Shit, that sucks," Jolie shakes her head. While we're walking she's just staring at her feet, at the purple shoelaces in her black Docs. Me, I'm staring up at the golden rain trees that have littered Jolie's street with yellow leaves.

"I keep wishing I had gotten to know him better, or paid more attention to his jokes, or something," I say. Jolie nods at me. I can't tell what she's thinking, so I go on, "Can you imagine dying today? Being hit by a car or a tornado while you're just sitting at home or something?" I can feel myself not breathing as easily, having to suck in large breaths to feel like I'm getting any air.

"Do you want to be cremated or buried?" Jolie asks.

"Ewww," I say, "Cremation is gross. Reducing a whole person to a pile of dust. That's terrible."

"I think it's cool," Jolie says. She would, too. "Did you know Janis Joplin had her ashes tossed over Marin Bay? I think I'd have mine flown up to the Arctic Circle and sprinkled over the ice or something."

"Then they'd just sit there, wouldn't they?" I ask, "They wouldn't, like, decompose or whatever, would they?"

"In the spring they would. I think."

"Well, I still think it's gross. And I'm sure Jason will be buried like normal." The words sound so weird. Jason will be buried. I picture him being stuffed under the ground still alive, still talking and making wisecracks while we throw dirt on top of him.

"Well, here we are," I say. I scrutinize the house. Pink shutters, ick. And these horrible green plastic chairs are on the front lawn. Someone was probably reading out here a few minutes ago. We go up to the front door and ring the doorbell. An older woman, older than my mom, answers the door with a pot holder on her hand and a brown business suit on.

"Yes?" she asks.

"Um, we...I found this," I hold the tags out, "I mean, I found your cat. She got hit by a car, I think."

"Oh Jesus, sweetie," she says, "Come inside, girls." We go inside a burnt baked potato smell. There's a pile of laundry in a laundry basket on the couch and evidence of a toddler strewn all around the house. Or maybe those are cat toys.

The woman lights a bent cigarette sloppily. I watch her suck hard on it to try and get it to burn evenly; then I glance over at Jolie, wondering what she's thinking. She's sitting intently at the end of the couch, as though every word this woman will say is of vital importance.

"That damn cat," the woman sighs, sort of sadly.

"We were thinking...we could help you bury him or something," I say.

"Bury him?" the woman asks. She touches her hair wearily. I notice she's got grayish roots, "I'm real busy tonight. I've got to finish making dinner for my entire firm, and my grandson is here while my daughter is at a convention."

I stare at her, flabbergasted. I guess it's obvious I don't understand someone not stopping everything they're doing to bury their own cat, because Jolie jabs me hard in my right hip with her bony elbow. I guess I was gawking.

"It's sweet that you girls came over here." She smiles. "What're your names?"

"I'm Jolie," Jolie sticks her firm handshake toward the woman. Jolie shakes hands like a man, that's the first thing I noticed about her in theater class. Not even just a boy, like a grown up man.

"Kate," I just kind of wave.

"I'm Rowena Lowenstein," the woman says, "Can I get you a soda or milk?"

"We really have to be going." I tug at Jolie's t-shirt.

"You must think I'm heartless," Mrs. Lowenstein says, looking surprised.

"You do what you have to do," I say flatly. I remember saying the same thing to Andrea when she returned from the hospital.

"I've got a lot on my mind," Mrs. Lowenstein says. Jolie is leaning back on the couch, surveying us both critically now. Jolie's cool detachment makes me more incensed with Mrs. Lowenstein for not reacting in the way I wanted, as though I have to be outraged for Jolie as well.

"I just wanted you to have these," I hand her the tags. I just want you to bury your cat, acknowledge that it meant something to you, acknowledge that you've lost something, is what I want to say. But you just want to leave the carcass to be eaten by possums or raccoons or get thrown in a dumpsite somewhere. We get out of that house as fast as we can. I guess Jolie can tell I'm really upset.

Back on the street, I feel free again. But my body feels heavier than ever. It feels like it wants to cry or scream or take a nap but it just can't.

The last fight

He likes to get even. "Your mom ruined you," he says. With a bitter feeling through my body, I usher in a grim smile. I feel as though I'm fighting myself to not cry, but tears stream down my face anyway. And with a mouse-like response, I say. "You're right" I look down; looking him in the eye is painful. With a profound sense of loss and resignation, I wipe my tears and walk away. He likes to win, and I just continue to break. I'm exhausted. He's gone now—really gone. And he left in the most profoundly inhumane way to me He left like the bullies I dealt with at school, in such a damaging way. I've added him to my list; you don't make my list easily. He doesn't care; I think he's dating someone new. I hurt him too, but not as catastrophically. I don't believe I kicked him like that; his intention was lethal. I keep rereading the texts; I like to hurt myself. I keep reliving it, hurting and hurting and spiraling and cutting. I use it to cry, hurt myself, or punch myself. It's like a grotesque game I play with my body and brain. Hurting and hurting and spiraling and cutting and punching and "UGhhh GOD!!" I screamed Stillness... I sighed I needed a breath. I sometimes wonder what it's like to drown in water. And I often times wonder what it's like to be him. The life of a toad, I want to be as selfish as him. Life just seems nice as an unknowingly tactless individual. It seems peaceful and calm. Stepping over people, warping their perception seems like a regular day to him. Seems like an unintentional afterthought, he did it not caring about the storm afterwards and the chaos after that. Reminds me of a big boulder just going over every tree in its path. Not really carrying about the collateral damage; the destruction is unbeknownst to him, and he doesn't care. At first I thought his actions hurt, but after uncovering the thought process. It's genuinely hard to look at. This shock I feel can only be felt when dealing with a true narcissist. I've never encountered one outside from her. This familiar feeling... I was incredibly appalled and heart broken. I was taken aback by the barbarity and incuriousness. It was like watching something disgusting on the street but then realizing it was happening to me. What did I learn from my last relationship? What it was like to be doted on, no matter how fleeting Some joy and security, even in the mundane, But he also taught me what it's like to be lusted after. It's important that I learn that. I will never get fooled into thinking it's love again. Those words are just words at the end of the day. Even if they're supposed to hold more gravity, not everyone thinks the same. But most importantly, he taught me what it's like to truly hate yourself. People sometimes throw insults at themselves, but they never truly resonate with them. When he berated me, his words almost broke me. I felt them deep within, and they became a part of me. I couldn't remember a time I didn't feel that way. But now I think...he's such a great teacher! I felt so much corrosion within myself—an infection. If I touched something, it would break down too. He really made me think it was mine. It never was; it was just taught to me by the best. Now I feel pity for this boy, stuck with such a crippling disease that he had to try and give it to someone else. He reminds me of my mom so much—fucking parasites. I see them now, and they're just so meek; you've got to cut them out quickly before they warp your perception. Is this what hatred is like?

The island of ennui I lay here on my island. My island is filled with an ocean of clothes, each with its own distinct character. Each fabric is a depiction of what once was and is now part of the ocean that lays on my floor. I lay here on my island, my blankets comfy but stale. Old and past, it's best years; I'm wrapped in them. I lay here on my island; what should I watch next? A movie? A show? doesn't matter. I'll still lay here, an unchanging log. I'm in two-week-old PJS, and while my island is safe and indulgent, it's rightfully suffocating. As I'm wrapped in these blankets, I can't help but think it's disguised. It must really be a choking snake, wrapping tighter and tighter around me. As I lay here on my island, I started to think, 'Is this the life I want?' Then, I take a hit. I smoke and see myself through the eyes of others; I can't help but feel disappointed. Although the high is here, the feeling of monotony won't disappear. What is my life? But as a constant

Eve Lyons is a poet and fiction writer living in the Boston area. Her work has appeared in Lilith, Literary Mama, Hip Mama, PIF, Welter, Prospectus, Poetry Quarterly, Barbaric Yawp, Word Riot, Dead Mule of Southern Literature,, as well as other magazines and several anthologies. Her first book of poetry, Tikkun Olam: Repairing the World, was published in May of 2020 by WordTech Communications. She works as an expressive arts therapist at an outpatient mental health clinic and teaches at Lesley University.

My name is Cierra Fillyaw, I'm 34 years old and I live in North Carolina. I've been doing photography since I was old enough to pick up a camera. My grandfather started me out with disposable cameras in the 90's. I love photography and the occult. Any chance I get to combine the two, I take head on.

Etsy:

IG: The_Occult_Co

FB: Cierra Des Os

TikTok: TheOccultCo

Michael Moreth is a recovering Chicagoan living in the rural, micropolitan City of Sterling, the Paris of Northwest Illinois.

A person sitting in a chair

Description automatically generated

Bobbi Sinha-Morey's poetry has appeared in a wide variety of places such as *Plainsongs, Pirene's Fountain, The Wayfarer, Helix Magazine, Miller's Pond, The Tau, Vita Brevis, Cascadia Rising Review, Old Red Kimono,* and *Woods Reader.* Her books of poetry are available at Amazon.com and her work has been nominated for Best of the Net in 2015, 2018, 2020, and 2021 as well as having been nominated for The Pushcart Prize in 2020. Her interests include cooking, knitting, reading, and pilates. Her website is located at

A close-up of a person

Description automatically generated

Tom Barlow is an writer of poetry, short stories and novels. His poetry has appeared in over 100 journals including *Ekphrastic Review, Voicemail Poetry, The North Dakota Quarterly, The New York Quarterly* and *The Modern Poetry Quarterly*. See more at .

A person with a purple headband

Description automatically generated

Toni Scales worked as a funeral director's assistant. Her poems have appeared in Lily, Wicked Alice, Stirring, blossombones, and The Pedestal Magazine. Her first poetry chapbook, Blue Rebecca, is scheduled to be published by dancing girl press. She lives in Bay City, Texas, and is excited about becoming a grandmother for the first time. In her spare time, she loves reading and watching psychological thrillers, and creating creepy doll pictures using AI image generations. You can contact her at toniscalespoet@gmail.com. For additional information, please visit .

A person with a beard

Joe Shaw prizefight2016@gmail.com

Joseph Shaw aka Cat Mack lives in Buchanan County, MO and works in management. He is an emerging writer with a love and passion for the horror genre and is also a horrorcore musician. He can be found on X under @JoeBloodsport.

A person in a black shirt and gray jacket

BIO: Terry Jude Miller is a Pushcart Prize-nominated poet from Houston. He received the 2018 Catherine Case Lubbe Manuscript Prize for his book, *The Drawn Cat's Dream*, and was awarded the Georgia Poetry Society's 2018 Langston Hughes Award. His work has been published in the Southern Poetry Anthology, the Lily Poetry Review, the Comstock Review, and scores of other publications including anthologies of the Austin International Poetry Festival, Rio Grande Valley International Poetry Festival, Texas Poetry Calendar, Chaffey Review, Houston Literary Review, Boston Literary Magazine, and the Birmingham Arts Journal. He is the creator of the Texas Poets Podcast. Miller is the former 1st Vice Chancellor of the National Federation of States Poetry Societies.Note about these poems: The lack of punctuation in my poetry reflects the way a person thinks...in flashes of understanding and comprehension...in lightning bolts of realization. This brings the reader closer to the poet while syllable count, word choice and stresses drive the emotions embedded in the poem...and more importantly...the reader.Twitter: @PoetTerryMiller Instagram: texaspoet

A person with a beard

James Croal Jackson <jamescroaljackson@gmail.com>

James Croal Jackson is a Filipino-American poet who works in film production. His latest chapbooks are *A God You Believed In* (Pinhole Poetry, 2023) and *Count Seeds With Me* (Ethel Zine & Micro-Press, 2022). Recent poems are in *Beltway Poetry Quarterly, The Lakeshore Review,* and *The Round.* He edits *The Mantle Poetry* from Pittsburgh, Pennsylvania. (jamescroaljackson.com)

A person holding a pen in his mouth

Description automatically generated

Dan Keeble hails from the furthest point East in the UK, and has enjoyed many successes with online and print publications of poetry, short stories, humour, and more serious articles. He has appeared in Fiction on the Web, Everyday Fiction, Turnpike Magazine, Scribble, Flash Fiction Magazine, Agape Review, and many others on a long journey to a stubby pencil.

A person smiling leaning on a ledge

Daisy Renee, was born and raised in a small town in Northern Arizona. When she is not scrubbing into surgery she can be found near a brook, pencil in hand, sculpting the essence around her. She originally picked up realism sketching a little over a year ago, when an extreme tragedy led her to an artistic breakthrough. The rest is history! Forever a girl with the imagination that brings fairies to life, and the talent to capture it.

A person wearing glasses and a jacket

Description automatically generated

Clyde Liffey lives near the water. Some of it is pictured behind him.

My X handle is @ClydeLiffey.

CB Adams, MFA, is a writer-photographer based in the St. Louis area. His analogue and digital photographs have been exhibited nationwide in more than 40 shows, purchased by an exclusive cadre of collectors, and published in Genre Urban Arts 7 and 13, Float, december, and Midwest Review, among others. Adams has received the State of Missouri's top writing awards – the Missouri Arts Council's Writers' Biennial and Missouri Writing! – and one of the top art awards as a Featured Artist. He has published more than dozen literary short stories and was named "St. Louis' Most Under-Appreciated Writer" by the St. Louis Riverfront Times.

IG: @qwerkystudio and @johnbent61

FB:

Website:

A person holding a knitted animal

Description automatically generated

I'm Layna Williams, a 26 year old living in Maryland. I'm a jack of all trades, master of none specializing in portraits and fiber arts. I aim to create something, anything, that captures the complexity of a child's wonder fighting for sunlight under the shadows of abuse. This pursuit brings a lot of strange, fun, and sometimes embarrassing ideas to life. Sharing them bring me a sense of purpose. Caring for houseplants and taking deep dives into various topics are my favorite ways to pass the time. Thanks for looking!

https://www.tiktok.com/@laynaslostart?_t=8nQCgOUBVAl&_r=1

https://laynaslostart.etsy.com

A person with red hair and piercings

Description automatically generated

Born on a new moon, on a Monday, in 1987, I grew up in a small town with small town thoughts and ideas. I come from a string of addicts and mentally ill, and I endlessly explore these ideas in my writing. I enjoy gardening, murder shows, cosmology and space, and caring for my family. My goal through writing is to carve out a comfortable place for people who may not have the words for how they feel. I was diagnosed bipolar at 19, and had a child the same year, after having a properly wrecked childhood myself. Despite this, all I'm searching for is peace and warmth to spread around. I'm becoming a certified mental heath peer support supervisor after 7 years on disability due to my mental illness. My story is one of clawing, gnawing, screaming, bleeding, hope.

-Elizabeth

Kelly Ann Wilson is a Canadian artist who captures the land and way of life around her in rural Ontario.

She comes from a family of artists, storytellers and dreamers and is following in the family tradition.

@kwilsonarts

My writing is featured on my writer's blog at:

https://kwilsonarts.wordpress.com/

A person with a beard and mustache under an umbrella

Robert Tustin is a writer whose work often delves into the intricate dance between chaos and structure. A poet by nature, Robert Tustin has recently started writing prose, crafting compelling stories and characters with a special interest in high fantasy worlds and the subtleties of human interaction. Originally from College Point, Queens, NY, Robert Tustin now resides in Myrtle Beach, where he is a manager at the local Barnes & Noble. He holds a Master's Degree in English Literature from Queens College, City University of New York.

Kendra Matott is an artist creating in Morgantown, WV. She transforms the mundane into the magical with her unique mixed media style--whether that's a landscape, one of her original characters, or a commissioned portrait. No matter the medium, Kendra strives to create images that evoke movement, mystery, and magic while balancing darkness with light. This duality inspired her art business name, Diabolical Whimsy. You can find more of her art on her website (), on Facebook (/diabolicalwhimsy) and on instagram (@kendramatott).

I'm Layna Williams, a 26 year old living in Maryland. I'm a jack of all trades, master of none specializing in portraits and fiber arts. I aim to create something, anything, that captures the complexity of a child's wonder fighting for sunlight under the shadows of abuse. This pursuit brings a lot of strange, fun, and sometimes embarrassing ideas to life. Sharing them bring me a sense of purpose. Caring for houseplants and taking deep dives into various topics are my favorite ways to pass the time. Thanks for looking!

https://www.tiktok.com/@laynaslostart?_t=8nQCgOUBVAl&_r=1

https://laynaslostart.etsy.com

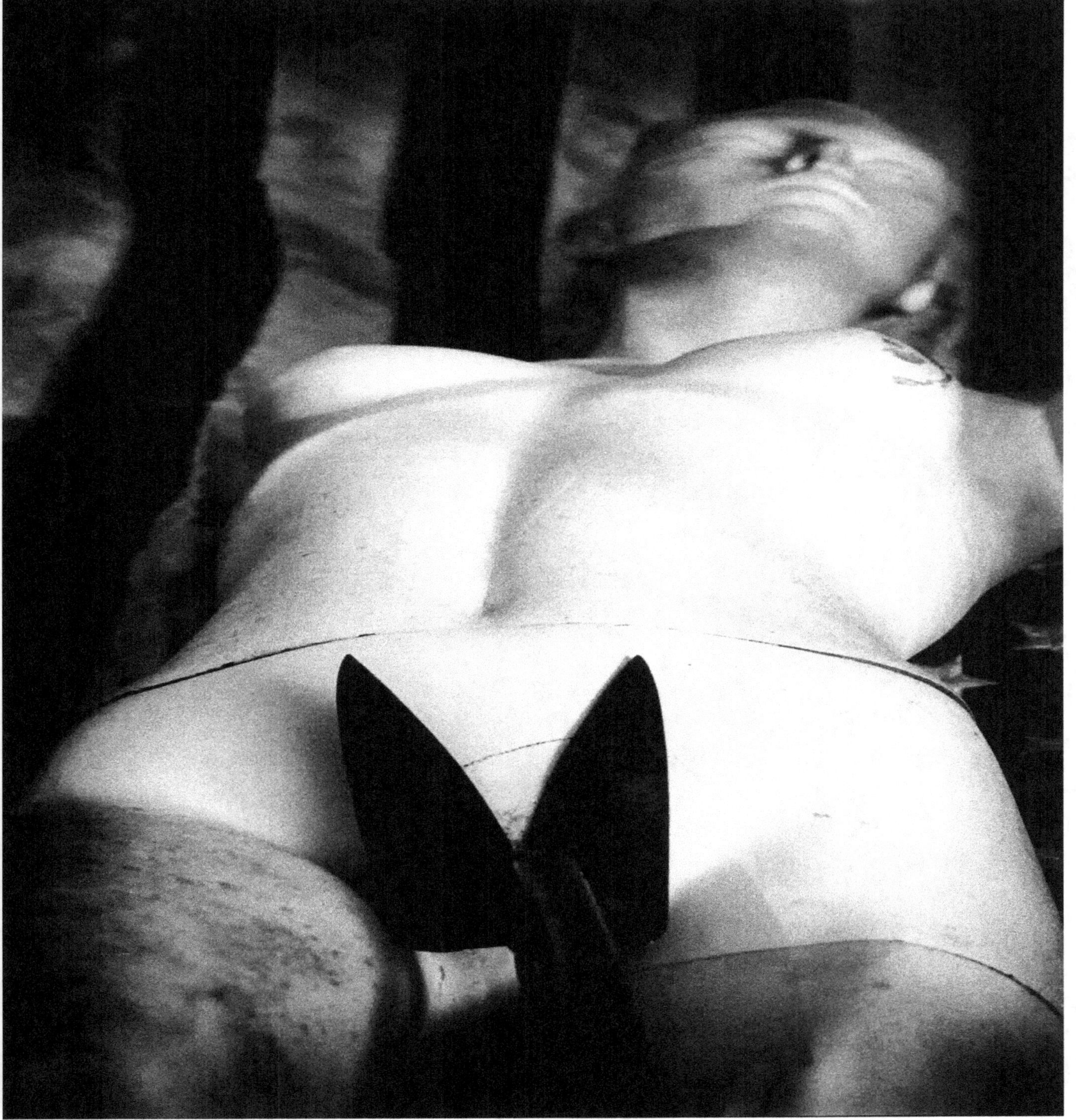

CB Adams